ABOUT THE AUTHOR

Aimee Alexander is the pen name of bestselling Irish author Denise Deegan. She lives in Dublin with her husband, two children and dog. Find out more on aimeealexanderbooks.com or tweet the author at @aimeealexbooks.

Also by Aimee Alexander

Pause to Rewind

The Accidental Life of Greg Millar

Checkout Girl

all we have lost

AIMEE ALEXANDER

ISBN-10: 1515250792
ISBN-13: 978-1515250791

All We Have Lost

Aimee Alexander is the pen name of Denise Deegan.
This book was first published as *Turning Turtle*.

In memory of my dear friend, Nicola Russell,
who inspired this adventure.

one

4pm. I'm at my desk, a desk so cluttered it's invisible. With my shoulder, I hold the phone to my ear while I slide a press release into a brightly coloured press pack already filled with 'relevant background information'. Only forty more to go.

Technically, I shouldn't be doing this. Technically, this is the job of a freelancer named Dick. I could have let his typo go – had I wanted to risk a lifetime of ridicule. Kim Waters, Pubic Relations Director. How many journalists would have spotted it? All it would have taken was one. My new title would have travelled fast. For evermore, I'd have been open to comments like, 'How's the old pubic relations going?' or 'I'm a bit itchy down there, Kim; I wonder could you have a look.'

I'm talking to a journalist now, trying to interest her in tomorrow's press conference. Line Two starts to flash.

'Sorry, Hazel, can I put you on hold for a second?'

Reaching to pick up the other call, my hand knocks against

my giant Wonder Mum mug. Cold, untouched coffee splashes out onto a silver-framed photo of my family and begins to ooze towards the press packs. I snatch them up just in time and land them onto an overflowing in-tray. I hold my beloved photo over the wastepaper basket as coffee streaks down my children's cheesy grins. Continuing to hold the phone to my ear I reach into my bag to retrieve a pack of hankies. Somehow I also pick up Line Two.

'I've got it!' announces my husband. What he's got, I assume, is the new job he's been after; what I haven't got is time.

'That's great, Ian! I *knew* you'd do it. Can I put you on hold for a sec? Sorry, hon.'

I reach for Line One but the light goes out before I can get to it.

'Actually, it's OK,' I say to Ian. 'She hung up.'

'A journalist?'

'Yeah.'

'Will I call back later?'

'It's grand. I'll get back to her in a minute and grovel.'

'Don't know how you do it.'

'You're not the only one.'

'So, how does it feel to be married to a banker?'

'You said the job was in corporate finance.'

'Which is a type of banking.'

'Let's just call it corporate finance. Live in denial.'

'I was thinking we could celebrate in Guilbaud's or are you up to your tonsils?'

It's our favourite restaurant but I find myself grimacing. 'I don't think I'll be out of here 'til at least nine. And I'm kind of knackered, to be honest.'

'We'll do it Friday?'

'Perfeck.' As we say in our house.

'Right, better let you get back to it.'

'Ian?'

'Yeah?'

'It was the lucky boxer shorts.' That I bought him.

'It *was* the lucky boxer shorts.'

'Seriously, though. Congratulations. I'm so happy for you.'
He deserves this. It's seven years since he took up his current well-paid, low-challenge job wanting to walk up the aisle a provider. When I later learned how frustrated he was, I encouraged him to move. When that didn't work, I nagged. Neither of us enjoyed that. So I let him be.

It's after nine when I pull up outside our home, a 1950s' redbrick in Dublin's coastal village of Dalkey. The outside light is on and coloured beams filter through the stained glass windows framing the door, making the porch warm and inviting. Water runs from the tub plants on either side of the door; the brass knocker shines. But upstairs the *Thomas the Tank Engine* and *Barbie* curtains are closed. Ian's car is parked where Sally, our child minder, usually leaves hers. Another bedtime missed.

I push the door in. All is quiet. I kick off my shoes and sink my feet into the rug. Its red, yellow and blue abstract shapes add colour to a hallway of white walls, wooden floors and modern art. The only sign of children are Chloe's bicycle helmet in the umbrella stand and two tiny pairs of boots by the door – bumble bees and frogs.

Ian appears at the top of the stairs, smiles and does a silent victory dance heavy on hip movement and air punching. In shirt, chinos, bare feet and gleaming wet hair, he's looking good. He dances his way down, then pulls me into a hug. I drop my bag and melt into him, inhaling his soapy scent.

At last, I pull back and smile. 'So, where's the bubbly?'

'I thought with the press conference...' He grimaces. 'Didn't get any.'

'Just as well I did, then. Damn, I left it in the car.'

'I'll get it.'

'I'll go up to the kids.'

'They're asleep. Sorry, I did try to keep them awake with *Rapunzel*. But it was just so late in the end.'

I nod. 'Were they asking for me?'

'Of course.' He kisses me. 'I told them you had a press conference.'

But all they'll understand is that I wasn't here. Again. 'I'll go up for a sec.'

Won't be long now before the pension, my legs complain as I mount the stairs. I remind them that they're only thirty-three. Then run the rest of the way up.

My smile, on seeing Chloe, is automatic. She's sprawled like a starfish, legs thrown out over the quilt, ladybird pyjamas riding up. Her foot twitches. The gentle light from her bedside lamp catches her hair, spread out over the pillow like honey. Sleep has relaxed her features, making her look younger than her four years. She turns over. Her thumb slips into her mouth and a finger curls over her nose. Sparkly pink nail varnish has begun to chip. I lean forward, brush a strand of hair from her face, kiss her soft, warm cheek and cover her up, knowing that her legs will be back out before I leave the room.

Next-door, Sam is lying on his back, arms tucked in by his sides, like a toy soldier that needs winding. His little cupid lips are open, white innocent milk teeth partially visible. He giggles suddenly but doesn't wake. I long to know what he's dreaming about. I make a mental note to ask in the morning. But can two-year-olds remember dreams? Sally will know. I kiss his forehead and gaze at him a little longer. Then I hear the front door close.

On my way back down to Ian, I catch my reflection in the gilt-edged mirror that hangs at the top of the stairs. It might be antique but it still works. Unfortunately. 'Efficient but exhausted,' is the look.

I find Ian in the sitting room, struggling with the champagne.

'Does someone need a hug?' I ask, actually needing one myself.

He puts the bottle down.

I propel myself into him.

'What kind of hug is that?' he asks, laughing.

'A body hug. You just force your body into the other person's body.'

'When you say force you mean attack with your stomach, you mean practically knock them over?'

'Well, yeah.' I step back. 'You try. It's fun.'

He starts off well but then, instead of forcing his tummy forward, he pushes out his upper legs and I lose balance, falling onto him. We collapse onto the couch, laughing. Then I stop because this is one incredibly cute hombre. Edible, really. I kiss him. He reaches for the buttons on my shirt. In the interests of balance, I reach for his. So, *this* is what I needed to unwind.

There is a good turnout at the press conference. The speakers are holding the media's attention. A group of photographers has gathered outside for the photo shoot and the bikini-clad models are turning blue while they wait. Any minute now the questions will be over and the shoot can begin. That's it. Last one.

I go outside as the photographer I've hired briefs the models. The press photographers take their places. Out of nowhere comes the theme song from *Mission Impossible*. A photographer reaches for his phone. Then another rings. And another. After a few uttered monosyllables, the photographers start to leave.

'What's going on?' I ask in panic.

'The body of a woman has been found in Blackrock.'

'Oh,' I say. What I really mean is, 'Oh crap.' We'll do our best, make sure each news outlet gets its own unique shot, creatively captioned and as soon as possible. But. The media like to use shots by their staff photographers. Our chance of coverage has just nose-dived.

I've all but finished clearing up when Ian calls.

'How did it go?' He always checks.

'Disaster.' I explain about the body.

'Hey, it's one press conference. They can't all be a roaring success.'

'True.' But try telling that to my client.

Two things combine to make me head home early. One: my job isn't exactly changing the world and may even be silly and pointless (I'm thinking bikinis). Two: Sam and Chloe were still asleep when I left this morning.

I make it home as they're finishing dinner at five.

'*Mum!*'

They spring from the table.

'Hey, guys.' I bend down, arms out and they propel towards me.

'But it's only dinner time,' says Chloe.

'I decided to come home early today.'

'Yay,' Sam shouts and body slams me. He inherited my hugging gene.

'Mind your suit,' Sally warns, as a lump of mashed potato from Sam's face is smeared onto my skirt.

'It's grand. I have to get it cleaned anyway.'

Sally dampens the corner of a towel and hands it to me. 'Right, back to the table and finish up, you two.'

They toddle back obediently.

I join them.

'Do you want yours now, Kim?' asks the child minder from heaven.

'No thanks, Sally. I'll wait for Ian. Listen, you go. Please. Grab the chance while you can.'

'They haven't had their baths yet.'

'Oh, well, *then*. You'd better stay. Go, go, go. Quick before I change my mind.'

She practically runs.

'So, guys.' I clap my hands. 'What'll we do now?'

They look at each other then back at me.

'Movie!' they shout together.

'What about your baths?'

'No one needs a bath *every* day,' Chloe says.

A convincing argument.

With Sam on my lap and Chloe curled into me on the couch, we experience seventy-seven minutes of what turns out to be great entertainment. I love these animated toddlers, even naughty Angelica – *especially* Angelica, who is a sass-fest. But no one beats Rex Pester, a tabloid hack who asks the mother of missing children, 'So tell me... how does it *feel* to know that you may never, see, your, children, again?'

'Where did you get this?' I ask.

'Sally. She said we can keep it.'

'Cool.' I reach for the remote. 'OK guys, bed.'

'Awwww.'

'Come on. It's late. You have to be up in the morning.'

'Can we just see da end of da moosic?' Sam asks.

'OK. But then straight up.'

I'm tucking them in when Chloe has something to share.

'You're like Angelica's mum.'

'Why's that?' I ask, thinking that she's definitely the most glamorous parent.

'Cos she's never there. The kids never see her.'

'Oh.'

'Yeah,' says Sam. 'She's always at wok.'

'Or on her phone,' adds Chloe helpfully.

Ouch. 'Well, I'm here now.'

'How about a story?' asks Chloe.

I smile. 'Didn't you just have a movie?'

'A quick one,' tries the uber-negotiator.

'Pleeeease,' Sam adds.

'OK, a quick one.'

I know I should be more like Sally – firm but fair – but it's just so good to see them. They do eventually sleep, which when it happens, surprises me – I'd begun to think they never would.

When Ian gets home, we ring the babysitter and head out for a walk and a chat.

two

Friday evening, we arrive at Guilbaud's. The maître d' welcomes us with a smile reserved for regulars and shows us to our table. En route, I take in the impressive, and no-doubt heavily insured, art collection. Passing a painting the size of a picnic-rug, my heart swells. It's like eating in an art gallery.

Seated now, I glance around at the other diners and see a few familiar faces – a leading businessman entertaining his large family, a celebrity dancer gazing into the eyes of her husband, and a (married) magazine editor with a handsome and much younger man who is not her husband. She acknowledges me with a smile and a 'let's keep this hush hush' look. She could keep it a bit more hush herself.

The sommelier fills our glasses.

I raise mine. 'To Mr Corporate Finance.'

Ian clinks his glass to mine. 'To Mr Corporate Finance; let's hope he can wing it.'

'Are you kidding? You'll be great.'

We sip champagne in happy silence.

'I was thinking,' Ian says after a while. 'Why don't we go away for a few days before I start? Sally could mind the kids.'

I've already thought of that. 'I have that bloody exhibition coming up again. I'm so tired of it, year after year.'

'Not to worry.' He looks thoughtful. 'Maybe I'll take a few days myself.'

'Do. Definitely.'

'Or maybe I should do some work around the house.'

I laugh. 'Hey, what do you call a group of bankers at the bottom of the sea?'

'I don't know. What *do* you call a group of bankers at the bottom of the sea?'

'A start.'

He smiles but weakly. 'Yeah, maybe less of the banker jokes.'

'*Why?* If you can't laugh…'

'Yeah OK but if we're out with work colleagues or something and you start having a go at bankers…'

'I *think* I'd know not to do that.'

'This is just a big deal for me. OK?'

'OK. Sorry. I just don't want you to turn into a banker. I don't want you to lose your sense of humour.'

'You see that happening?'

I smile. 'Actually, no.'

'Well, then.'

'I don't know why we're even talking about work. We never talk about work.'

'True.'

Our starters arrive. They, too, are art. Almost a shame to eat them. Almost.

'Who would you like to be if you could be anyone else?' Ian asks.

I think for a moment. 'Me?'

He smiles. 'Good choice.'

'What about you?' I ask.

'Bill Clinton.'

'Bill *Clinton*!'

'He has a great personality, is really intelligent *and* he gets laid a lot.'

I laugh. 'You get laid a lot.'

'This is true.'

'OK, I'd like to stay me but maybe do something mad.'

'Like what?'

'I don't know. Pack it all in.' I have *no idea* where that came from.

'You're joking, right?'

'Right.' I think.

'Phew.'

'Why phew?'

'Because you'd hate being at home all day.'

'Would I?'

'You've always said so.'

'This is true.'

'Anyway, you're great at what you do.'

'It's not exactly rocket science, Ian.' In fact, I could do it in my sleep. Which is half the problem. The challenge has gone. And there's that novel I fantasize about writing...

'Anyway, I'm not permanent yet,' he reminds me.

'I know.' It would make no sense.

The weekend is a typical one, the claw-back-family-time agenda organised with military precision:

06.30 hours: rise and shine, dress children, breakfast together

09.00 hours: trainspotting

09.20 ride on commuter train

10.05 battle to get son to leave train

10.10 calm restored with treats – all round

10.11 realise bribery is probably a mistake

10.15 return to base-camp. Fight temptation to put on *Thomas The Tank Engine* and return to bed

10.20 tooth-friendly refreshments and play on garden swings
11.00 emergency first-aid
11.02 Thomas video
12.30 healthy, nutritious lunch
13.45 lunch ongoing
14.30 Dublin Zoo
17.45 Dad makes dinner while Mum bathes children
19.00 estimated time of sleep
19.45 actual time of sleep
20.00 arrival of babysitter and exit of parents from family home for essential recovery

Sunday morning's agenda is interrupted by urgent replacement of the bathroom window.

I stand in the bathroom and look out at the very hot workman.

'Hel-*lo*. Ian, isn't it?'

'Mm hmm,' he replies, balancing on the ladder, a nail in his mouth.

'I *love* having workmen around the house.'

He takes the nail slowly from his mouth and smiles like a man in a Diet Coke advert.

'Makes me feel safe,' I add.

He starts to pull his T-shirt over his head and I worry he might fall.

'I should go mind my children.'

'Yes. Why don't you do that, you dirty slut, before your husband finds you flirting with an innocent window-fixer.'

A throat clears.

Ian looks down into the next garden, smiles and gives an awkward wave. 'Hey, Tom.' He turns back to me and grimaces.

'I love you,' I whisper.

Monday, my friend, Sarah, wants to meet for lunch. Says she has news. Sarah usually does.

'So, I'm leaving *Girlfriend*,' she announces. *Girlfriend* is Ireland's best-selling women's magazine.

'But it's one of the best publishing jobs in the country. And you're such a good editor.'

'I want to write.' She pulls on her e-cigarette like it's oxygen.

'You already do.'

'Novels.'

I told her it was my dream. She said nothing at the time.

'You *know* what age I am,' she adds.

I'm one of the few that does and have been sworn to secrecy. Heading for forty, she looks ten years younger, dressing with confidence and always provocatively. It's all done with careful deliberation. Nothing about Sarah is an accident. Even her hair matches her personality. She wants to be a redhead, so she is. If she were an animal, she would be a lion.

'Isn't it impossible to get published, though?' I ask. It's why I haven't tried. 'Shouldn't you try it in your spare time first, in case it doesn't work out?' At least she *has* spare time.

'Actually. I *have* been.'

'You kept *that* quiet.'

She waves her hand. 'I was just faffing about. But now I've lined up a publisher.'

'*How*?'

'Met an editor at a party.'

She's unbelievable. Succeeds at everything she does. Everything.

It hits me, suddenly – if you want something to happen, you have to make it happen. You have to believe in yourself and take the leap. Yes, she's chasing my dream. But at least, she's doing it. And she's making me see that it will never happen for me unless I do the same.

'You know who you remind me of?' I ask.

'Who? I think!'

'Jackie Brown, you know, from that Quentin Tarantino movie?'

She frowns. 'Jackie Brown is black.'

'Yeah but you have her sassiness, her sex appeal….'

'Sex appeal, you say?'

'I do.'

'Must watch it again. Pick up a few tips.'

'You don't need tips.'

She leans in close. 'OK, so, this is top secret but I've pitched another idea to my editor – and he likes it.'

'What idea?'

'I'm going to travel the world in search of The Perfect Man and record my exploits for a non-fiction work, while finishing the novel. What do you think?'

'Wow.'

'I *know*!'

'So you're really going?'

'I leave next week.'

'For how long?' I ask incredulously.

She shrugs. 'As long it takes.'

'I can't believe you're only telling me now.'

'Only decided this weekend. Booked the tickets this morning.'

'And you'll never go back to *Girlfriend*?' It was great having her in there in terms of placing articles.

'Hope not. They've given me a year's leave of absence – so that safety net is there if I want it. They know they can't do without me.'

'What will *I* do without you?'

'Miss me?'

I think of her travelling the world alone. 'Be careful, though, yeah? Don't go anywhere dodgy.'

'Where would the fun be in that? The book has to be entertaining, Kim.'

'The book won't exist if you're dead.'

She smiles. 'I'll be fine; I'll have you worrying for me.'

'Yeah, that'll really protect you.'

'I'll keep you posted on all my exploits. You'll know where I am at all times.'

'That's what I'm afraid of.'

She laughs deep and throaty like Jackie Brown.

After lunch, Maeve, arguably my most career-minded client, greets me with her traditional hug and air-kiss routine in the lobby of the multinational she works for. Cleopatra without the asp, Maeve sports a severe black bob, Roman features, perfect posture and zero expression – she doesn't like to give anything away, not even her state of mind. She could be beautiful – if only she'd smile. Immaculately groomed as ever, and ten minutes late, also as ever, she walks me to her office. Marketing accolades fight for space. Nowhere is there a potted plant, photo of a loved one, postcard, funny pen…. A private eye's worst nightmare – no hint of a life outside the office.

'So,' she says, once we're seated. 'We seem to have achieved reasonable coverage.'

She's referring to the press conference. And she's wrong. We got tremendous coverage. But this is Maeve Boland whose chosen method of motivation is the withdrawal of praise. The technique is this: make everyone work harder in case, one day, she might actually bestow a 'well done' upon them.

'I was pleased with it, especially considering the murder,' I say.

'Hmm. We didn't get on the Morning Show, like last year.'

'That's the point; we got on it last year so they didn't want to go again so soon.'

'Hmm. Anything we could have done better?'

I remind myself that I don't need this business. I can walk away at any time. 'Don't think so, no.'

'No room for improvement at all?'

She could improve her attitude. But I don't point that out.

'Right. Well.' She passes me an agenda, then looks down at her own copy. Opposite the heading, 'Press Conference', she places a neat tick. She lands the tip of her Mont Blanc on the second bullet point and looks up. 'Let's talk about a PR strategy for the rest of the year.'

Let's not, I think. 'Do you have a written brief?'

'Well, I thought we could discuss it now.'

That would be right – on my time.

I force a smile. 'So. Are we targeting the same audience as usual?'

'Latest research suggests we're on target. No reason to change.'

I nod. 'Could I have a copy of that research? It would help in developing a strategy. How about the product messages? Any reason to change those?'

'Again, they seem to be impacting the target market. Brand awareness is ninety-five per cent. Of course, advertising is responsible for most of that.'

No doubt she's saying the reverse to the ad guys. I control an urge to sigh, yawn, stretch, walk around her office, jump up on her desk and dance. I am heroic.

'So,' I say. 'The only reason to change anything, then, would be competitor activity. Anything I should know?'

'Nothing significant. I'll e-mail you what I have.'

'Great. Budget the same? Or are you increasing it?' My own private joke, just to cheer myself up. I know the answer.

'No. No increase.'

'Right then. If I've any questions I'll e-mail.'

'Or call.'

So she can talk for hours, milking my brains? No thank you.

Though we're technically finished, Maeve manages to drag the meeting on. And I don't, to my credit, get visibly angry, pull her hair, leave prematurely, or kill her.

As soon as I'm out, I call Ian and arrange to meet for coffee.

He calms me down, makes me laugh and I pray that he'll be as available when a bank owns him.

three

Every day, before noon, I'm guaranteed a 'quick hello' from Ian. Today, it doesn't come. It's his first day in the new job and I'm dying to know how it's going. I could call him but don't know his direct line, if he has one. I could ring his mobile but don't want to interrupt a potential power meeting with his new boss. I could call AGT Corporate Finance and go through reception. That would leave a great impression – the new boy's wife is on the phone; can't survive a few hours without him.

So I wait.

I come home early (six) so I'm there to greet him.

No need, it turns out. He's late (eight).

'How did it go?' is my new welcome home.

'Fine. What's for dinner?'

'Sally's chicken curry.'

'Great. I'll just go up to the kids.'

'They're asleep. Sorry. I kept them up as long as I could.'

He smiles. 'Role reversal.'

He goes up to them anyway.

'So?' I try again when we sit down to eat.

He zones in on his curry like he hasn't eaten in a year.

'Ian. You started a new job today, remember?'

'Vaguely.' He smiles.

'Should I ask a series of multiple choice questions or are you just going to tell me how it went?'

'Probably best to ask the questions.'

I shake my head sadly. 'OK. What's the place like?'

'Fine. Modern.'

'Have you your own office?'

'Yep.'

Blood from a stone. 'What's it like?'

'Fine. View of Stephen's Green.'

'Do you've a secretary?'

'A communal one. Probably won't use her much.'

'What's your boss like?'

'She's all right.'

'*She?*'

'Yeah. Actually, Kim, I'm kind of shattered. Let's talk about your day. How was it?'

'Boring.' Seeing as everyone's being honest.

We're silent.

I should just say it, the way Sarah would. A dream is a dream. I can make it happen. Here goes.

'How would you feel about me taking a career break?' OK, so Sarah would have made it an announcement, not a question.

He frowns. 'A career break?'

'Yeah from PR.'

'For how long?'

'I don't know. For good, maybe?'

'Then it wouldn't be a career break.'

'No.'

'What would you do instead?'

'Maybe write a novel?' I straighten, annoyed with myself for the 'maybe'.

'This wouldn't have anything to do with Sarah, would it?'

'Ian, this may surprise you, but I do have a mind of my own. I wanted to write a novel long before she did.'

'It's just all a bit sudden.'

'I've been thinking about it for ages.' And talking myself out of it every time.

'But writing *a novel*, Kim – what makes you think you can do it?'

'What makes you think I can't?'

'There's no need to get defensive. You know I've every confidence in you. What would you do with the business, though?'

I shrug.

He raises his eyebrows. 'You'd just walk away from a lucrative business? With no agent lined up? No publisher? Do you even have an idea for a novel?'

The answer, we both know, is no.

'Shouldn't you try it out first before giving everything up?'

'It's not just about writing. It's the kids. They don't know me – not really. I'm the woman who sees them before they go to bed (on a good day) and is nice to them. I don't even get cross like real mums in case they stop loving me. They run to Sally when they fall. Ian, it's time I got my priorities right.'

He looks at me for a long time. 'OK. Let's talk about our options,' he says like we're in a business meeting.

'What options?'

'Well, what about letting some of your clients go and using the extra time to write and see more of the kids?'

I feel my body tense. 'That would be OK if I *could* carry on in PR but I can't, Ian. It seems so pointless. So irrelevant. So stupid.'

'What's got in to you?'

'Nothing.' Burnout, maybe.

'OK, what about selling the business? Build it up and sell it on. You could make a fortune.'

'I can't wait that long.'

'Why not?' His voice is impatient now.

'I just can't do it any more. I'm tired of plugging Flush toilet cleaner to the world. How excited can a person get about sunscreen, year after year? Life's too short, Ian. Do you know what age I am?'

'Thirty-three – not exactly ancient, Kim.'

'I could be dead next year.'

He smiles.

'Well, I *could*. And how would I feel, breathing my last, knowing that I didn't make the most of my final year on earth?'

'And what if – as I sincerely hope you do – you live to be eighty-seven?'

'Well then, well then… When I finally do die, I'd like to be able to look back over my life at all the things I'd done and say, "Yes, I have *lived*. Yes, my children *knew* me."'

He smiles. 'Then, do it.'

'Really? You think I should?'

'Yeah I do.'

'But you're not permanent yet.'

'Well, you could always think about it for a bit longer.'

'Right. OK. I'll do that.' Now that it's a possibility, it has become suddenly scary.

9am and already there's a message from Maeve asking me to call her urgently.

Though it kills me, I do it.

'Oh, Kim, great! You got my message?'

'You said it was urgent?'

'Yeah, I was ringing about the proposal you presented yesterday. It's a little light on activities, isn't it?'

That urgent? 'That's all the budget allows, Maeve. If you want to increase it, I can by all means add more activities.'

'I'm sure we did a lot more last year for the same price.'

I take a deep breath; then count to five. 'Let me pull out last year's proposal. Actually, why don't I call you back?' I don't need to look at last year's proposal; I consulted it when preparing this one. Contrary to what she thinks (or would have me believe she thinks), I'm not trying to screw her. I make myself a coffee. I check Twitter and the morning's newspapers for mentions of my clients. After fifteen minutes, I call her back.

'Maeve, looking at last year's activities, I realise that I've under-budgeted this year's proposal.'

'Oh. Really? Wow. OK. Well, I can't increase the budget, Kim. It's fixed. My hands are tied.'

I push back a cuticle. 'All right, let's leave it at that then but we'll have to revisit it, next year.' The thought that I mightn't be around gives me the sweetest thrill. And just to remind myself why I mightn't be around, I flick through the proposal I've just presented to her.

Activity No. 1: Press Conference – Caffeine is Good For You – new research.

Activity No. 2: Celebrity endorsements – sponsor celebrities to be seen and photographed in public with client's drink in hand.

Activity No. 3: Photoshoot – Twelve Green Bottles (life-sized) Hanging On A Wall with twelve Big Brother contestants pushing them off.

Activity No. 4: Sponsor university rag week.

Activity No. 5: Mother's Day competition on daytime TV.

Once we get over the budget issue, Maeve claims to love the proposal. I wonder if I can spend a year implementing it. I'm particularly depressed about Activity No. 3. How did I come up with it? I'm slowly losing all credibility with myself.

People like Maeve are actually great, though. Because they make you think. Things like: life's too short; I'm selling myself short; if only my working day was really short; and what a short fuse I have. I can taste freedom in the air. I imagine days spent writing, not listening to her, not editing and re-editing her press releases then changing them back to the original, not reassuring her, not appeasing her. Just making up stories. Stories where people follow their dreams, where mothers can be with their children, where the main character can quit and still win.

I know now. There's no way I'll ever be able to carry out my proposal for Maeve. Maybe – subconsciously – I made it so ridiculous on purpose, knowing that I could never be able to go through with it. I can't do this to myself any more. I need to believe in what I do, in myself. I need a challenge. I need to be with my children. I need to quit.

Ian will be made permanent. And I'll become a bestseller.

four

If kidnapped by aliens, blindfolded and returned, I'd know I was in my mum's kitchen by smell alone. The reassurance of home baking; I could do an article on it. Or not.

Mum looks at me as if I have, in fact, agreed to take off with aliens.

'But why?'

'I'm tired, Mum.'

'Tired?'

'Yes, tired. Tired of having to think up news angles and PR proposals for non-newsworthy, boring products. Tired of writing creative captions for pictures of cheesy businessmen in grey suits. Tired of having to be gung-ho about Flush bloody toilet cleaner. I'm tired of being enthusiastic.'

She's wearing her understanding smile but I know she's no clue what I'm talking about.

'I know you've been a bit busy lately but I thought you loved PR. You've always said it's the best job you've ever had.'

'It was. Not any more.' I sigh. 'It's my own fault. I've been working too hard for too long. I just can't do it any more. D'you know how many weeks' holidays I've had in nine years?'

'How many?' It's a regularly expressed concern of hers. She's probably got them counted.

'Nine. One a year. And maternity leave?'

'You *know* how I felt about that. I still can't believe you insisted on bringing your phone into the labour ward.'

'Kim Waters PR – contactable between contractions.' I roll my eyes at myself. 'I'm just too busy, all the time, no let up. The phone is always ringing. Clients always want more. The kids need their mum and, since Ian started his new job, we're both home late most evenings. It's not a life.'

'That's desperate. I didn't realise you were under such pressure.' She reaches across the table and squeezes my hand. 'You must stop.'

I let go the breath I seem to have been holding for a very long time.

'Spend more time with Chloe and Sam.' She smiles. 'And that lovely mother of yours. Oh and don't worry about the cooking – I can give you loads of recipes.'

'That's what I'm afraid of.'

She laughs. But persists. 'How about my Bolognese sauce? You all love that.'

'Let's start with that ready-made sauce you mentioned that you just add to pasta?'

She hesitates. 'Usually I add bits and pieces to that, to give it texture – a few chopped peppers, mushrooms…'

'But I *could* just stir it in as it is, couldn't I?'

'You could but…'

'Sure, I'll start with that. Thanks.'

She gives me a jar to get me going. I turn it around in my hand, automatically wondering who does their PR. I dismiss the thought.

'Let me give you the Bolognese recipe as well. It's so easy.'

'Mum, if I do quit, it'll be to write a novel and spend time with the kids. I won't have time for culinary delights. Just the basics.' Enough to keep starvation at bay.

'Really? A *novel*?' asks my mother the reader, recipe forgotten. I nod.

She clasps her hands together. 'You've always *loved* books. Oh Kim this *is* wonderful news. What kind of novel?'

'A murder mystery, I think.'

She covers her mouth. She's a crime fan, the gorier the better. She leans forward.

'Have you any of it written? Can I've a little peep?'

'I haven't started it yet.'

'Oh,' she says, a little deflated but by no means put off. 'And love scenes? Are there going to be any love scenes?'

'You mean SEX scenes?' It's good to scare your mother, occasionally.

'You know what I mean, you monkey.'

Thirty-three and she still calls me a monkey.

'I don't know. There's not a lot of passion in murder mysteries, is there? They're more plot-driven, aren't they?'

'Well, maybe you should have just a little one.'

I love this woman.

Then I think of her – and everyone I know – reading the 'little' sex scene and projecting Ian and me into it. I shiver.

'I've such admiration for you,' she says. 'You've always done your own thing. You're great.'

I grimace. '*Is* it the right thing, though, giving up my independence? It's not really me, is it?'

She considers that. 'Well, you've always valued your independence but it would be a mistake to let it hold you back. Don't let it stop you from following your dream.'

Wow. She's starting to sound like me. Only it makes more sense when she says it.

'You're lucky to have Ian's support. Lean on it for a change. You supported him to go back to college and you weren't even married then. Anyway, it won't be for long. You'll be producing bestsellers in no time.'

Mum's dangerous. Tell her you're about to jump off a cliff and she'll be right behind you, cheering you on, thinking of all the ways she could possibly help.

'What's the worst that could happen?' she asks.

'Ian isn't made permanent?'

'You could always get another job.'

'You have a point.'

'There's a reason you're sitting in my kitchen.'

We smile.

'Thank you, oh wise one.'

'You're welcome, Grasshopper.'

five

D-day. Today, I break the news to my clients that I'm winding up the business. How, though? I've a nine-year relationship with my favourite client, Frank. That's longer than I've been married.

I should start by getting out of bed.

There, over the first hurdle.

Stuck at the second, though. Can't decide what to wear. Not my favourite red jacket. Too cheery, too aggressive to bring down the axe in. Better to hide behind charcoal grey. I look in the mirror and wonder what I'm doing – turning my back on a great income, security, independence. I've no agent, no publisher, and no idea for a book. It's not too late to change my mind.

Sam wanders in, sporting a ruffled just-woken-up look, as he does twenty-four-seven. He'll know what to do.

'Sam, say yes or no.'

'No.'

His favourite word. We can therefore disregard it.

'Ian, tell me I'm doing the right thing. I mean it's not logical, is it?'

No answer, though I know he's awake.

At breakfast:

'Chloe, what do you think?'

She examines me seriously then puts down her Coco-Pop-filled spoon, squints at me, then smiles like she has an answer. 'Sea horses, Mum.'

Okaaay.

One last attempt at Ian. 'What do you think, honey?'

'I *think* I'm late for work.' He stands, grabs a slice of toast, pecks my forehead and heads for the door, flinging his tie around his neck to be knotted, en route.

My 'Bye' comes out as a sigh as I watch him disappear down the hall. He trips over an Action Man truck, but – heroically – keeps going.

Then, it hits me. *That* is what I have to do. Keep going. Stick to the plan. Go after the life I want. Anything else would be selling my soul.

Frank is first on my list. I take one last look around his office before breaking the news. His Yucca plant is as disinterested as ever. His geometrical screen saver is gyrating at the same slow pace. The blatantly branded coffee cups are looking a little sad but that's nothing new. I realise that life will glide on without me.

And so I get to the point.

He leans back in his chair, face impassive. He folds his arms.

He thinks me mad. He sees my invoices. He knows what I earn.

'Well, fair dues to you, Kim. Just going for it. To hell with the consequences.'

Really?

'We all dream,' he says dreamily.

I wonder what his is.

He sighs. 'But Mary's not working. I've the mortgage to think about, school fees, pension plan....'

Suddenly, I feel on the edge of some great adventure. I am Sinbad. I am Jules Verne. I am still terrified.

Maeve suddenly sees me differently.

'Where'll I find someone as good as you – and at your rates?' She taps her pen against the side of her forehead. Repeatedly. 'Are there any agencies you'd recommend?'

Suddenly, I feel sorry for her. 'I'll have a think.'

She squints. 'Are you *sure* you want to do this? It seems a bit drastic.'

I nod.

'Shouldn't you have a stab at the writing first just to make sure it's for you?'

I smile. 'Probably.'

She thinks for a moment. 'OK,' she says then, like she's granting me permission.

I wonder about the people in her life. Is she like this with them, too?

'Would it be all right to call you, occasionally?' she asks.

'If you're stuck, I guess.' But basically NO.

'You're giving me a month's notice of course…'

'Of course.'

'Good. Good.' Then she looks at me for a long time. 'I'll miss you, Kim.'

Suddenly, I'm humbled.

The rest of my clients take the news almost disappointingly well. I arrive home in a state of mild shock that I've done it. Actually taken the first step towards changing my life. I send Sally home for the day and hug the kids.

We make Rice Krispie buns with Jelly Tots on top. And eat too many.

Ian arrives with a bottle of Moët and a 'body hug'.

I get emotional. 'I didn't think you cared.'

'Of course I cared. I just had to let you decide for yourself.'

'But the decision involved you too.'

'I had to step back, Kim. You kept changing your mind. One minute you wanted to quit and that was fine by me. The next minute you didn't, and that was fine too. But when you kept switching, I started to stress. With every change of mind, you were changing our future. I had to stop listening.'

I grimace. 'If it's any consolation, I was driving myself mad too.'

'No. No consolation.' He kisses me. 'Congratulations! You've done it. Now, let's get on with our lives.'

I look at him and worry that I am asking too much of him. 'You *are* happy about this, aren't you?'

'Do you want me to kill you?'

I laugh. 'Sorry.'

'Look, Kim. As always – if you're happy, I'm happy.'

I smile. 'I am. I'll make this work. I promise.' Writing is my new career. I'll treat it as such. Nothing will get in my way.

He raises his glass. 'To the next Agatha Christie.'

'God. Couldn't you pick someone more contemporary?'

'Well, I don't know. I don't read crime.'

'Patricia Cornwell.'

He tries again. 'To the next Patricia Cornwell.'

My glass is a sword I raise to the sky. 'Let the adventure begin.'

six

A month later, I exit the world of PR the same way I entered, quietly. No big party. No grand finale. I hate letting Sally go. Worse, I hate that the kids will be separated from her. She promises to babysit. And I promise myself I'll be the best mum ever.

Work commitments evaporate. Mornings free at last.

At the kitchen table, I face a blank screen. And can't decide. Should I plot the whole thing out first or just start writing? I heard or read somewhere that you should start with a character – an interesting character – and give him or her a dilemma.

Given that I'm writing crime, I decide to go with plot. I need one that's never been done before. I root around in my brain. Without success. I pace the kitchen. They say that every plot is in the Bible. I should get a Bible.... Actually, I should buy a book on writing. And some crime novels.

I go straight to Amazon. And browse. Who'd have thought there would be so many books on writing? It reminds me of the gold rush; the people making the money were the ones selling the shovels.

I can't decide on my shovel.

I check my emails. There's one from Sarah – who I still haven't told. Ironically, I didn't want her to think I was copying her.

So I email her. She replies instantly, wishing me luck – and calling me a kept woman. To Sarah, relying on a man would be like selling her soul in a mail order catalogue. It's not something I'm shouting about either. But it's temporary. Like going back to college. Or losing a job. It's a blip. And it's character building. How much more rounded will I be having faced rejection from publishers? Because there will be rejection. I'm not naïve enough to believe otherwise.

It occurs to me that my inbox is crowded with emails I no longer need. Browsing through such subject headings as, 'Head-above-the-rest mousse' and 'Just Smell It,' I wonder how I did this for a living for so long. A lovely thought hits: I don't need to deal with this any more. I delete the most recent. Bing! Instant freedom. Bing, bing, bing! An actual buzz. Only one thousand-three-hundred-and-eighteen to go. Maybe I should keep some excitement for tomorrow.

An email from an old, dear friend reminds me of his existence. I should never have stopped sending Christmas cards. How many others have I forgotten? Connor used to be my closest friend before I met Ian. We told each other everything, shared promises. My friend became our friend. The kids arrived and time, well, it evaporated.

I reach for the phone.

He laughs when he hears my voice.

And it's like we never lost contact.

'Interesting,' he says of my news.

'Define interesting.'

After a pause, he asks, 'What are the chances of getting published, a hundred to one?'

'Shut up.'

'Actually, a hundred to one is probably optimistic.'

And still he manages to wangle a dinner invitation out of me. For later today.

'So eager,' I say.

'Just a lazy chef.'

'A word of warning: you *have* sampled my culinary delights in the past.'

'I like to live dangerously.'

As soon as I hang up, Ian calls with a newsflash. O'Donnell Haskins PR has just been sold to an international firm for fifteen million euro. It's all over the business pages. I try to remember helpful suggestions from the numerous self-help books I've devoured over the years. Don't look back. Ne regrette rien. *Feel the Fear and Do It Anyway*. I didn't want to build an empire and sell it. And yet, a nest egg would be nice. Especially a nest egg that size. Kim Waters hacking back undergrowth in the Amazon basin. Kim Waters breaking the sound barrier. Kim Waters opening a funky art gallery.

The phone call stimulates an urgent return to the computer. And Amazon. I pour over books and finally end up buying five – three on writing, one on finding agents and publishers, and a crime novel that catches my eye.

Once more, I confront the empty screen. I should start with a title. Titles sell books. *Eats, Shoots and Leaves*. The title sold that book.

Or maybe I should start with the ending, so I know where I'm going.

I put on music for inspiration.

I make coffee for stimulation.

I hear the post arrive. Maybe the walk to and from the front door will trigger something.

I open the post.

Bills, mostly.

I try to think of a brilliant twist. But to have a twist you need a story.

I make another coffee.

I check Twitter and Facebook for possible inspiration but, really, I'm procrastinating.

My alarm goes off. I stare at my phone in horror. The morning's gone! I have to pick up the kids! I can't believe it!

A quick analysis of my first day as a writer reveals the following:

Word count: zero

Plot: non-existent

Characters: unborn

Title: *Murder…*

And I'm not sure that the word 'murder' in the title isn't a bit obvious.

But it *is* good to see their little faces, to be there for them as they burst out into the sunlight, to pick them up and swirl them around, to feel their arms around my neck, to hear that they love me.

We go to the park and have ice cream.

We watch a DVD together.

I feed them at five like they're used to. We chat. No rush now. Just time.

I bathe them in 60% bubbles, 40% water.

Putting them to bed, I nuzzle Sam's tummy. Chloe screams when I tickle her. Their love is so physical, so huggy. When finally they sleep, I'm not far behind. But it's a different kind of tired than I'm used to. A satisfied kind.

I go downstairs to put on fresh pasta. The laptop sits on the kitchen table like a dare. I remind myself that it was my first day. It'll get better. Once I get started. Once I have momentum.

I'm stirring in the non-homemade sauce and trying to think of titles when Ian arrives home. Hungry.

I sense his disappointment when he sees the pasta. He says nothing just grinds a lot of pepper onto it. I'm passing him the Parmesan when the doorbell rings.

'Oh my God! I forgot Connor!'

'What?'

'I invited Connor to dinner.'

Ian looks down at it as if to say, 'not much of a dinner'.

And I forgive him. Because he's right.

Standing at my front door, Connor looks very Christian Grey. Expensive suit. Equally expensive hairstyle. His smile hasn't changed, though. And he hugs the same.

He holds up a bottle of wine. 'Brought your favourite.'

I examine the label. 'Ah yes, excellent year.'

'You'd swear you *knew* something about wine.'

'I know more than you.' Though that wouldn't be hard. Connor doesn't drink. Can't. 'Come in. It's so good to see you.'

In the kitchen, Ian stands. 'Connor.'

Connor produces a smile and a casual wave. 'Ian.'

'Sit down,' I say. 'Connor, it's either pasta or pizza.'

He takes one look at the pasta. 'Pizza.'

'Good choice,' Ian says.

I hit him. Then hand him the wine to open while I turn on the oven and take the pizza from the freezer. I go to the fridge.

'Connor, I don't have Coke. Sorry. Will juice do?'

He smiles. 'You forgot I was coming, didn't you?'

I grimace. 'Sorry. It was a weird day. New routine and stuff.'

'How did the first day's writing go?'

'Did a lot of... thinking.' Even that seems like an exaggeration.

'Always the best place to start,' Ian says.

And I feel like weeping in gratitude.

'Have you thought about what you'll do if the writing doesn't work out?' Connor asks.

'Jesus, Connor! A bit of faith!'

'Just wondering if you have a Plan B, that's all. The publishing world's in shit, isn't it?'

'I won't need a Plan B. I'll get there.'

'You could run an art gallery! *That,* I can see.' Connor tips his chair back as his eyes wander the kitchen, taking in the paintings. 'Cool gallery. Lots of oils. And sculptures. Those chunky bronze horses you love. Abstract human shapes. I can picture you now, deciding how to hang your latest collection, allowing your customers to browse, then pouncing just at the right moment.'

'I sound lovely. Like a vulture. Anyway, you're missing the point. There is only Plan A and it's a novel.' I go get his pizza.

'Bet the kids are glad to have you home, though.' Connor looks around. 'Where have you hidden them?'

'They're in bed.'

'So early?'

'They were tired. *I* was tired.'

'How are they? They must be pretty big now.'

I could tell him that Sam likes to throw things in the loo and he's not fussy what. Or that Chloe makes 'art' out of her food. But he's a single guy; there's a danger of boring him to death.

'They're grand,' I say. 'It's so good to spend time with them.'

'It is so you, though, isn't it, the whole art gallery idea?'

'Enough with the art gallery.' I look at Ian who, I realise, isn't saying much. I clear away his unfinished but abandoned plate. 'Connor, Ian got a new job.'

Connor turns to him. 'Oh?'

As they discuss the intricacies of corporate finance, I try not to think of my wasted morning. Or Plan B. A time will come when I'll look back on this day and smile knowingly, having achieved everything I set out to. 'Ah, remember those early days of doubt, how you had to order a small library of books to learn how to write and how friends doubted that you could do it. Well, you showed them.'

'A toast,' Connor says, raising his orange juice. 'To the corporate financier and the novelist.'

It sounds sexier than it is, I think as I raise my glass. Then I catch Ian's eye. He winks as if to say, 'We can do this.' He has always had a special ability to read my mind.

seven

The following day, I start with motive. This actually gets me going. By twelve-fifteen, I have a – kind of – plot, half a wobbly first chapter and an entire title. There is something a little iffy about *Murder She Said* but I can't quite work out what. I'm not worried; it's a working title.

I collect the kids from Sunny Side Up, their effervescent Montessori – feeling pretty effervescent myself. We head to Sandycove's tiny beach. It's only March but the sun smacks off the water as we pull up.

'Shearave,' Sam says, from the back of the car.

'She's a rave?' I offer uncertainly.

'Sheawuff,' he insists.

'See the wolf?'

'No-oh. Seedavave.'

'See the *wave*?'

'Yeah. Seedawafe. Told ya.'

'Yes, yes, I see the wave!' I exclaim, so relieved at hitting the jackpot that I ignore the fact that the sea is, in fact, calm.

I unstrap them both and lift them out of their car seats. I walk them carefully to the beach. Then they take off, tearing headlong into the freezing water fully dressed. Too late to do anything, I let them play. When I do manage to get them out, I wrap their shivering bodies in towels I brought for feet. I will learn.

Next morning, I become borderline unhinged. Chloe won't get out of bed, no matter what I say about mutual back scratching, general co-operation and Montessori. Sam wants Cornflakes having already requested and been given Cheerios. Chloe's persistent chant of, 'I want Sally back,' makes me want to bang my head against the wall.

'Will you put the bin out?' Ian asks.

I stare at him. 'You haven't even unloaded the dishwasher!'

'So?'

'They're your only two jobs.'

'Yeah well, this morning I don't have time.'

He hasn't had time any morning this week. 'What about my time?'

'Kim you're at home all day.'

'Yeah, working. Writing.' Or trying to.

'Look, I gotta go.'

'Go, then,' I snap. Is this my future – cleaning up after everyone while the caveman goes out to track down the deer and antelope?

He's not too happy that I'm not too happy. Leaves for work in a huff.

I've just brought out the bin, when he rings from the car.

'I'm sorry.'

I take a deep breath. 'It's OK. It's just you *know* how sensitive I am about turning into a doormat.'

'I know.'

'And you *know* I'm writing. I haven't actually given up work.'

'Yeah.'

'And it takes time.'

'I know.'

'And I have to squeeze everything else into the rest of the day.'

'I know.'

'And being a mum is a full-time job. Sam, stop.' He's spooning soggy Cornflakes onto the table.

'I know.'

'And the thought of emptying the dishwasher day after day gets me down.' I don't mention the cooking.

'Kim, I'm calling to say sorry.'

Sam is whacking his cereal with the back of his spoon, sending it flying. 'Sam! Stop!'

'Kim, I'll do the dishwasher, all right? I'm sorry. OK?'

'Sam, don't you dare.'

He tips the bowl over. Cereal and milk oozes over the table and onto his lap.

'I gotta go.'

'OK. I'll call you later.'

I lunge, right the bowl and slide the cereal into it with the side of my hand. 'Sam, that's *bold*. I *told you* not to.'

'You given me *two* headaches,' he says.

'Do what you're told in future, young man.'

I unstrap him and lift him out of the seat. I carry him upstairs to find that Chloe has dressed herself.

'Good *girl*!' Maybe I'll survive another day.

I change Sam and hurry back downstairs to get Chloe's breakfast and another for him. How did Sally always look so unruffled? How was she always so cheery? And how did she get them to Montessori on time? I should have paid her more.

I ignore the mess in the kitchen and open my laptop. I read over the one-and-a-half chapters I've written. Overnight, it has become unoriginal and clichéd. I reach for the phone.

'Oh, hello, love. I was just going to ring you.' Mum says this every time I call.

'Well?'

'Well what?'

'Did you read the first chapter?'

There's a pause. 'I haven't really had a chance yet, love.' Weak, very weak.

'Mum, you've been dying to get your hands on it.'

'I've just skimmed over it.'

'And?'

'Maybe we shouldn't discuss this over the phone,' she says as though the lines are being tapped.

'OK. When do you want to do it?'

'Eh, let's see.'

'I can come over now.'

There's a pause. 'All right, Kim. Just give me half an hour.' Her voice is resigned like she knows when she's cornered.

I shouldn't go. I don't need any negativity, right now.

Still, I have to know.

She makes coffee and talks about the children in minute detail. My tongue is hanging out and my head feels like a good pat. There comes a point when I can't bear it any longer.

'So what did you think of the chapter?'

'Goooood.'

'What's wrong with it?'

She starts to twiddle her pearl earring – always a bad sign. 'Don't you think the title is a bit like *Murder She Wrote*?'

'*Murder She Wrote!* I *knew* it reminded me of something. That's grand. I'll change it.' Easily. 'Is that all you were worried about?'

'Well, no.' She grimaces. 'It's probably not ideal, is it, that I've worked out who's going to be murdered?'

'Not in Chapter One, no.' But maybe she's wrong. 'Who do you think it is?'

'Gerald?'

Shit. 'How did you know?'

She shrugs. 'There are just so many people who would want him dead.'

My plot is suddenly sounding very Agatha Christie. 'Maybe it doesn't matter,' I say hopefully. 'He's killed off in Chapter Two.' Or at least he will be when I get into Chapter Two a bit more.

She starts to look like she's in pain.

'*What?*'

'I might have figured out the murderer.'

'You couldn't have! Who?'

'Grace.'

Oh. My. God. 'How did you *know*?'

Super sleuth explains.

I drop my head into my hands and groan. 'This is a disaster.'

'Kim, I do read a lot of these.'

'So do most people who read crime.' I stand up.

'Where are you going?'

'Home to fix it.'

'You can't go. Not like this.'

'Like what?'

'Upset. You'll crash the car.'

I roll my eyes like a teenager taking her frustration out on a parent.

She follows me into the hall then passes me out and stands blocking the front door.

'What are you doing?' I ask.

'You're not leaving until you promise me you're not upset.'

'I'm not upset.'

'You are.'

'Jesus, Mum, will you let me out of here? I'll drive safely. OK?'

She looks at me carefully as though she can read the future of my journey home.

'All right.'

'Thank you!'

'Kim?'

I turn.

'Sorry. I wasn't going to tell you till you were further along.'

'Well, that would have been crap. At least I can fix it before I waste any more time.' Fix it? I'll have to come up with a whole new plot. Start over. I feel like going to bed for an extended period of time. Possibly a year.

Driving home, a voice inside my head asks, 'What made you think you could write a novel?'

'Nine years' experience of PR writing, some of it very creative,' another answers.

'Not the same thing as a murder mystery, though, is it?'

'I've done some very good articles. Remember the one on feet?'

'*Feet!*'

'Anyone who can make feet sound sexy can write a book that's mysterious.'

'Not looking good so far. Just saying.'

'Where would we be if the Wright Brothers believed the sceptics or Leonardo da Vinci decided he should stick to the painting or Christopher Columbus was afraid of falling off the edge of the world?'

'Don't get carried away. It's just a book.'

'Exactly! It's just a book. Doable. Entirely possible.'

'Just focus on the goal, Kim. Visualise it.'

'Better wait for a red light, though.'

It's nearly noon already. No point starting now. I check my emails. There's one from Sarah. I'm not sure I'm in the right frame of mind. Curiosity wins out.

Hello missus. Having a ball here in Sydney but time to move on. The Aussies aren't bad for a quick sexpresso but no sign of Perfect Man. Right now, I'm thinking New Zealand, then Kenya. Thoughts? My first novel, **The Other Woman,** *will be out in July. And I'm flying with Piece a Cake. Title inspired by the process of writing. How's it going with you? Sx*

Thoughts? Here's a thought. She makes me feel like poo. Here's another: I've reverted to the mental age of two. Next day, though, I do it. Start over.

eight

My brother, James, is getting married in New York. Ian and I are going – on our own – for a long weekend. There *is* a God! Unfortunately, He doesn't renew passports. I have just – miraculously – discovered that mine will expire when I'm due to be over there. Not wanting to impinge on a morning's writing, I wait till I've picked up the kids to start the process. While they eat (and wear) their lunch, I fill out the form. Then it's off to have my passport photos taken. Looking straight ahead is an extreme challenge as Chloe struggles to keep Sam safely inside the booth. He starts to scream. We narrowly avoid a meltdown.

Then it's in and out of car seats. A trip to the police station to get the photos stamped is followed by a longer journey to the passport office. Treats are supplied en route. All is going reasonably well until we have to queue at the passport office. My self-help books say that my two-year-old is becoming his own person, learning that he is independent of me. I am to ignore bad behaviour, reward good. The book does not advise on what to do when the two-year-old lies on the floor of a public place, arms and legs flailing, pushing his vocal chords to the limit.

I give him my phone. And Chloe gives me a very adult look. My children are turning into the characters in the books I read them – Horrid Henry and Perfect Peter. I don't want them to be either horrid or perfect. Then again, maybe they could both be perfect – just for a day.

My phone starts to ring as I carry a sleeping child through the front door. I lay Sam onto the couch, knowing that he won't sleep tonight but not feeling up to waking him.

I take out my phone and call Mum back.

'How much have you written now?' she asks.

'Three chapters.'

'Send them to Deirdre French,' she says, referring to a bestselling Irish author who happens to be a friend of hers. 'I'm sure she'll be able to give advice, tips, whatever. This is her email. Send what you have as soon as you hang up.'

'OK, thanks.'

But when I do hang up, I sit down on the couch and pull Chloe up onto my lap. 'Sorry about all the waiting, today. You were such a good girl.'

'Was I perfect?'

I press her nose. 'Perfect. But I don't want you to feel you have to be perfect all the time. Cause that's a lot of pressure.'

'No it's not. Sam is bold so you need someone good.'

I hug her. 'He'll grow out of it.'

'He better.'

Three weeks later, my mother is asking if I've contacted Deirdre French to see what she thinks of the chapters.

'I thought I'd give her a bit more time,' I say.

'Ring her.'

Her persistence wears me down. After a motivational mug of coffee, I dial the number she's given me.

'Ah, hello, Kim darling,' the author says.

'Hello, Ms French.'

'Deirdre, please.'

'Deirdre. Thanks so much for having a look at my... (writing, work, what?)... at what I've done so far.'

'I hope I can be of some help.'

'Mum thought you might have some advice...'

'How *is* your Mum?'

'Good, great. Getting ready for New York. James is getting married there.'

'Ah, lovely. So what can I tell you? Let me see. Have you got a pen?'

I reach for one. 'Yes.'

'Good. Take this down.'

'Thanks.'

'Writing's a business. Treat it as such.'

I scribble 'a business'.

'Write two thousand words a day, every day. No excuses.'

I write '2,000', wondering how many pages that is.

'You need a good strong central character.'

'That would be the detective?' I confirm.

'In your case, yes.' Deirdre French writes romantic fiction.

Conscious of her own two-thousand-word deadline, I get to the point. 'Would you have any advice on plot?'

'Ah, people get way too uptight on plot,' she says, as if I've touched a nerve. 'Now, about your work,' she says, pointedly, as though conscious of her own deadline. Given the publishing phenomenon that she is, I wonder how much each of her words is worth.

'Thank you,' I say, pen poised.

She sounds very encouraging as she breaks the news that what I've written 'needs work'. My plot is 'leaky', my characters 'one-dimensional', my vocabulary 'pedestrian'.

I put down the phone. And cry.

When I recover (it takes a while), I open my laptop and do a word count. Five-thousand-eight-hundred-and-two words.

According to Deirdre French, this should have taken me three days. It's been four weeks. And it's pedestrian.

'Deirdre French thinks my book is crap,' I say to Ian.

'She really said it was crap?'

'Well, she didn't actually use the word. But she meant it.'

'I'm sure she didn't. Wouldn't.'

'She's right, though. It *is* crap. *You* think it's crap too. You just won't admit it.'

'Kim, you know I don't read fiction.'

'I know, but you must have *some* opinion.'

'And it's this: better no advice than bad advice.'

'I've given up my business for nothing.'

'Kim. Deirdre French is one person.'

'Yeah, but she knows what she's talking about.'

'Does she write crime?'

'No,' I say grudgingly. I feel two-year-old grumpy.

He smiles. 'Come here.' He opens his arms.

I snuggle into him. And feel marginally better.

'You'll do it. I know you will. You're great.'

'You're biased.'

'I know. I'm your biggest fan.'

I start to smile. He pulls me closer.

'Pretend we're in a cave and there's a blizzard outside.'

'It's you who should be writing books,' I say but I do it – I pretend we're in a cave and there's a blizzard outside. It's lovely.

I stand in front of an open case. Six condoms for three days? Call me an optimist.

We park at the airport. I'm raring to go but the (official) worker of the family has to make three 'quick' work calls first. I've no problem with that – easy to be positive when there's a mini-break on the horizon. I take out my copy of *On Writing* by Stephen King, but get a little distracted by the man beside me. He's got the most gorgeous profile. I sit forward to get a peak at his eyes, my favourite Ian feature – it's the way they change from blue to turquoise depending on the sky.

He hangs up.

'What are you looking at?' he asks, smiling.

'You, Ian.'

'Me, *Tarzan.*'

'You Ian – as opposed to You Dad or You Husband.'

'And yet I do have quite a number of Tarzan-like features,' he says swishing back imaginary long hair.

'No loincloth, though.'

'That could be arranged. Come on, Jane, let's go.'

'I'll just grab my vine.'

We walk in sync towards the airport terminal. I bump him with my shoulder. He bumps me back and I go flying. We laugh and he holds out his hand. Taking it, I tell myself that I shouldn't worry so much about the writing. I have Ian. I shouldn't forget that. I can lean on him, a little. He won't mind; he might even like it.

About an hour into our flight, Ian gives me a corny smile. He takes my hand and begins to, what can only be described as, 'fondle' it. Then he starts to serenade me. Out loud. On a full – and very big – plane.

'Every time you go away,' he sings, earnest and cheesy. 'You take a piece a me with you…'

I'm laughing when an airhostess arrives with a *Financial Times* for the crooner. He doesn't drop my hand or look awkward, just beams up a very charming thank you.

She looks at him as if to say, 'You can serenade me any time.' Then walks off.

'She remembered,' he says, touching his heart.

'Either that or people were begging her to do something – anything – to stop the "singing".'

He gives me one of his earphones so that we're still together while he reads the paper. I reopen my book. The sun catches the diamonds on my engagement ring and I make the three little dots dance on the clipped-up tray in front. I fold away the armrest and slip my legs over one of Ian's. Cosy.

Thirty-three is probably old to join the Mile High Club. (Boy, those loos are small.) And it's probably not cool to become a member with a spouse. But, getting off the plane, we're one condom down. And grinning.

The wedding is a cosy affair. Bride and groom look like they've leapt from the last page of a fairytale. Mum looks fabulous, dressed in a beige suit, elegant in its simplicity. Her wide-brimmed hat is the definition of understatement, her only flamboyance being a few more pearls than usual.

I stand up too early to deliver my reading and have to sit back down again. When I do step in front of the microphone (and entire congregation) I trip over words like firmament – mostly because I swore I would.

Relieved it's over, I return to my seat beside Mum. When the you-may-kiss-the-bride moment comes, she holds my hand.

'He'd be so proud,' she whispers.

These are the worst moments, the ones that Dad would have hated to miss. I put my arm around her. I hate that he is missing this, but decide to be grateful, at least, that he was there for the happiest day of my life. He never did get to meet his grandchildren; didn't even know they were coming. I learnt I was pregnant with Chloe the day after he died. He would have liked to go out on a positive. At least, though, we had something to focus on, look forward to, live for – especially Mum who was thrilled to be chosen as Chloe's godmother.

The day flies. But we have Sunday. And that's all it takes to regress to the pre-parental stage – chatting, laughing, messing, walking, kissing, touching. Lots of touching.

We do leave the room – to eat. New York's sights are kept for another time.

I wonder how we can hold on to this holiday-romance feeling when we get home. More time together, out of the house, on our own. Meeting in town after work. Stolen afternoons in the penthouse of the Clarence Hotel. They've got a hot tub. There *is* the issue of money and the fact that I'm not making any. And Ian's not yet permanent. Only one thing for it: I have to make this novel work. I have to make a living.

On Monday, we say goodbye to Mum who is staying on for a few days with her new in-laws. I hug James, then Rachel, but can't leave without a warning:

'Don't rush into anything.'

'What? *Kids?*' James asks.

I nod. 'Give it five years.'

They laugh.

'Kim, we've been together seven already,' says Rachel. Her eyes give her away. I used to be like that, thinking, 'we won't let children change our lives' and 'we won't call each other Mum and Dad' and the big one, 'we'll do it differently'.

'I wish you wouldn't talk like that about the kids,' Ian says in the taxi to the airport. 'It sounds like you're sorry we had them.'

'You know that's not what I was saying.'

'What, that you love them but if you were to do it again you wouldn't have had them?'

'No. Just that they shouldn't rush into it. They should have some fun first. That's all.'

'What if Rachel is already pregnant?'

Oh crap. 'You don't think she is, do you?'

He shakes his head.

My mind starts to race. 'God, I hope they *can* have kids.'

'I'm sure they can. Stop worrying.'

'A person doesn't stop worrying just because another person tells them to.'

He kisses me. 'Try.'

'I *am* glad we had kids. You know that, don't you?'

He smiles and kisses me again. 'Course I do.'

At JFK, while Ian sits with a copy of *Fortune*, I track down presents for Sam and Chloe.

'You think you've got enough?' he asks when he sees all the bags.

'There was just so much good stuff.' And, OK, a bit of guilt.

Smiling, he shakes his head.

Walking to the car in Dublin, we're holding hands. Though I'm dying to see Sam and Chloe, I can't help thinking about the trade off – bye, bye intimacy. That's when I decide that it doesn't have to be like that. I just need to take control.

As Ian drives, I take out the notebook he bought me for my writing. I start to make a list.

New Me Resolutions:

1. Get organised – make lists.

2. Get fit – bum firmer, tummy tighter and hips, well, smaller.

3. Shoulders back, chest out, tummy in. Remember, posture is camouflage.

4. Get romance (i.e. sex) back on track. Work on strategy.

5. Ignore all bad behaviour – I will, I will, I will.

6. Reward good – especially my own.

7. Arrange more time for self – be firm.

8. Have fun.

9. Chuck self-help books.

10. Think before opening mouth.

This will be the new me. I promise.

nine

On Sarah's advice, I send my – edited – first three chapters of what I'm now calling *Peripheral Fear* to her literary agent, Tessa Browne. Weeks pass. Slowly. After six, as advised, I call her.

She gets to the point.

'The writing is patchy. Some bits are good,' she says cheerfully, 'some not so.'

I don't ask for the ratio. Her comment on the plot helps me out though:

'It's been done to death.'

'Oh.' My stomach plummets like mercury in a thermometer.

'Writers have to put in a lot of hard work. It's a very difficult life.'

'I see.'

'Advances have fallen sharply. It's not a good time to be starting out.'

Somehow, I don't think she said that to Sarah.

'If I were you, I'd stick to the PR. Much more lucrative.'

I hold it together till I hang up.

Then – with disastrous timing – Sarah rings.

'You OK?' she asks. 'Tessa just called to say you guys had spoken.' There's a pause. 'She can be a bit… abrupt.'

I'm mortified, wondering what she said to Sarah about what I've written.

'Don't let her stop you. That would be a mistake.'

'Maybe she has a point. Maybe I'm just not good enough.'

'Why don't you open with a sex scene? Get people right into the story.'

I close my eyes. And breathe.

'Books sell on the first chapter, Kim. A good sex scene and you have them. Guaranteed.'

'Right.'

'Actually, why don't you write *erotica*?'

Silence while I struggle not to outright bawl.

'I'll write it for you if you like.'

'It's OK, thanks. How's Australia?'

'New Zealand now, mate,' she says in a Kiwi accent. 'And I've met him – Perfect Man!'

'Really? So soon? Wow! Who is he?'

'Maori. The real thing. Staying power of an ox.'

I laugh. 'So that's the end of the book, then?'

'God, no. Why would it be?'

'Well, you found him. What's there to write about?'

'Oh, he'll be the last chapter. I'll have to continue my research for the middle of the book.'

'Right.' A pause. 'Won't he mind?'

'He won't know.'

'Until the book comes out.'

'I'll deal with tomorrow tomorrow. How's that sexy husband of yours?'

Scary when she talks about Ian in those terms. 'Grand.'

'Kids?'

'Yeah, fine.'

'Give everyone my love.'

'OK. And Sarah? Thanks, you know, for the introduction. Hope I didn't waste her time.'

'Least she could do. I'm making her a fortune. OK, gotta go. There's a man, here, that needs my attention. Ciao, hon.'

'Bye, Sarah.'

I need to lie down.

The kids are off today so I'm up at six, researching erotica. I'm wondering if I have it in me when I hear whispering and light footsteps on the stairs. I click out of full-on steam.

I go to the door and watch them toddling downstairs in their PJs. They are holding hands.

'Shh,' Chloe says.

Sam puts a finger up to his mouth.

Ah, God.

'Good boy,' she says, like she's the mum.

Into the kitchen they pad, partners in crime. Chloe climbs up on a chair to open the fridge. Sam places his order. She starts to pass it down to him. A yoghurt. A tomato. Cheese. Healthy, I'll give him that.

I reverse into a corner of darkness as they bring their picnic into the sitting room. They turn on the TV and flick through the channels until they find cartoons. It doesn't matter to them that the voices are in Irish, a language they haven't yet learned. God, I love kids. Not just my own.

I open the laptop. And a completely new file. The mouse blinks at me, expectantly.

Right.

I'll have a stab at a sex scene. Can always delete it.

I start out OK but when I get to the actual *act,* mortification hits. I am confounded by terminology, uncomfortable with words like 'throbbing member' and 'dewy mound.' There are children in the room! Even if there weren't, I'd have the same problem – because the general idea is for people to read this.

I hear Ian getting up. I scan what I've written. And blush. It's a biology lesson.

I've wasted an hour!

I delete every embarrassing word and am faced, once again, with a blank screen.

Maybe I should open with a murder. Something shocking. Unusual.

I press my fingertips into my temples. I crane my neck. Yawn.

I hear the pump come on for the shower upstairs. Desperation rises. I can't think.

My tummy rumbles. I long for toast.

Then, suddenly, I have it! Electrocution!

My fingers take off over the keyboard. All around me fades.

'Oh. They're watching television,' Ian says, like they're slitting their wrists.

I take him in, all dressed up and somewhere to go. This is how I must have looked to Sally – the over-compensating parent. How easy it is to be right when all you have to do is give instructions and walk out. Not so long ago, I saw television as an unnecessary evil. Now I know it's a necessary one. The day is long. Start with a hive of activity and you run into trouble of the cranky-tired variety. Ian doesn't know that. He's still the working parent. Explain to him, Kim; it's part of your job description now.

'Ian, they're having such fun. They got up by themselves, sneaked down and helped themselves to food. They're getting on so well because this is their little secret. But here I am, sitting in the corner, keeping an eye.' I see him soften, so finish off with, 'Don't worry. I have it timed. One hour. That's it.' I don't say, 'Now off you go, your conscience is clear,' but that doesn't mean I'm not thinking it.

And as I watch him leave, it hits me that this is not the first time since I quit work that he has tried to tell me how to parent. My heart flutters. He is *not* in charge. We are still a team. Equal.

As the car pulls out of the drive, the hunt begins for my

notebook, specifically my list of new me resolutions. This is suddenly important.

After a desperate hunt, I find the notebook behind the couch with a crayon. My list – and most of the notebook – is covered in green scribbles, Sam's favourite colour. I run my finger under each line of my list. What can I do that's immediate?

No. 3. Posture.

I straighten up, shove my shoulders back and raise my chin.

No. 9. Chuck self-help books.

Not sure I can do that. It would be like throwing away my safety net. Plus, they were expensive.

But I am determined.

I round them up. It takes a while.

Throwing them out would be sacrilege. I'll trade them for some crime novels in our local second hand bookshop. Then I'll bring the kids for a walk on the pier. That's three resolutions in one day. Go me.

I arrive at the bookshop with a carrier bag of advice on how to live a happy, adjusted, rewarding, positive, sex-filled, fun, tantrum-free life. And wait for the man behind the counter to finish with another customer.

'Guys, stay here.' What is so fascinating about the door? 'Hey, look, children's books over there. Have a look.'

It works.

I have the man's attention now. He pulls book after book from the bag, doing a quick tot. After about the seventh how-to guide, he sneaks a look at me. His expression gives nothing away. Do I look desperate or cured?

'I'm perfect now,' I laugh awkwardly.

He doesn't react, just goes back to the job at hand. Why did I bring them all in together? Twenty-two self-help books; I could have set up in competition with him. He continues to dip in and pull out. I turn to check that Sam and Chloe are not dismantling his shop. The guy behind me in the lengthening queue looks away when I catch him staring at my books. I look at his. Oh, *Atonement*. Right.

I notice that all my good posture from earlier has gone. I feel a sudden need for books that are no longer in my possession – not badly enough to have to ask for them back, though. I leave the shop with two brand new children's books, which have used up most of my credit. I take a deep breath. To the pier, my lovelies!

Fresh air. Ah yes. This was a good idea. People pass by, mostly women, some strolling, others powering along. Many are in pairs, chatting animatedly. I long suddenly for an adult conversation. For a friend. Sarah seemed more than enough when my schedule was tight. I could ring Liz, a journalist I used to meet for lunch occasionally. But spending more time with the children has made me realise: I don't have a lot in common with Liz. Not really. What I need is a new friend. Someone in my position. What am I talking about? I have two thousand words a day to write. I know; we'll go see Mum.

ten

Mum takes a home-made quiche from the oven and I think it must be true that the smell of baking sells homes – I instantly want to move in. Chloe, carrying salt to the table, decides to tip it into her mouth. Sam looks at his sister and reaches for the sugar. I take the salt from Chloe and move the sugar out of reach.

The arrival of food makes things easier.

The quiche is so good it silences us.

Until finally, Chloe says: 'I'm full.'

I look at her plate. 'Just two more spoons, then bring your plate to the sink and you can go outside.'

'OK, Mum.'

'I full too,' says Sam on hearing the word 'outside'.

'Let me feed you for a sec, then you can go out with Chloe, OK?' Never have my days required such a level of negotiation.

Out onto the patio they troop and into the sandpit Mum has bought to entertain them when they're here. We watch through the open patio doors.

'How are things?' Mum asks.

'OK. Not as easy as I thought they'd be.'

'It's a big change. You need time to adjust.'

'It's just that I thought that *the writing* would be easier. I just can't seem to make any progress.'

'Maybe you need a break.'

'I took one yesterday to paint Sam's room. While I was doing it I actually seemed to get some good ideas. So I abandoned the painting, went to the laptop and typed like crazy. Then the Montessori rang to tell me I'd forgotten to pick up the kids. I forgot my own children. Sally would never have done that.'

'Sally wasn't writing a novel. At least you got some ideas for the book.'

I shake my head. 'When I got back to the computer, I realised that what I'd written was complete rubbish.'

'Some of it must have been good.'

'No. None. The paint must have made me high. It was off-the-wall.'

She smiles. 'How's the room?'

'Sam loves it.'

'There you go. Don't be so hard on yourself. You're a great Mum.'

I half smile.

'Why don't you take a break from the writing for a while? Maybe you've got…what's it called…writer's block?'

'Or maybe I'm just crap.'

'Well, you're not going to make any progress feeling like that. Take the summer off. Allow yourself time to adjust to the changes you've made to your life. You've just given up running a business because you couldn't do it all. Now you're replacing the business with a novel while still bringing up a young family and keeping a home. Ease into it, love. Soon they'll be getting holidays. Why don't you stop now and wait till they go back in September to start again. You'll be in a better frame of mind.'

'But I can't just give up now. I've only been at it three months.'

'You have your whole life. Don't always be in a rush. Enjoy the kids. Trust me, Kim, they grow up very quickly.'

'But I have to earn an income!'

'And you will,' she says calmly. 'But you're getting nowhere at the moment. You're just tying yourself in knots. Step back. Have a special summer, one that you'll never forget, let the inspiration come to you and when the kids go back in September, then start writing it all down.'

I nod. Maybe she's right. Maybe I should just let it come. Stop trying to force it. Press releases were so much easier. I miss the short deadlines, the immediate results. I miss sending out invoices and getting paid. This is just so broad and fuzzy. It feels like I'm getting more and more lost.

'Apart from the writing, how are things?'

'OK.' I look out at the kids. Sam's sporting a builder's bum as he loads sand into the back of a pick-up truck. Chloe is sifting sand through a strainer while bossing her family of Baby Born, a mangy monkey and Buzz Lightyear. 'Sometimes, I feel like I'm falling through the cracks. I don't have a career and I'm not exactly an earth mother. I don't really fit in anywhere anymore.'

'Why don't you go back to tennis? You used to have a great serve. Tennis clubs are great for meeting people.'

'Maybe when I make a little progress on the book.'

'Don't try to do it all, Kim.'

'Right.'

'Have you spoken to Deirdre French?'

I try to throw her off the scent. 'How do you know each other anyway?'

'We were in secretarial college together.'

'What's she like?'

'Smart. Ambitious. She wanted to study English but her parents didn't have the money to send her to college so she got a job in a publishing company and pretty soon convinced them she could write.'

'I remember reading that somewhere.'

'Probably when she had a book coming out,' Mum says,

uncharacteristically cynical. 'I'm not sure I'd completely trust her. I hope you didn't tell her too much of your plot.'

'I've abandoned that plot.'

'Did she give you any tips?'

'Yeah. She was pretty helpful.' I share some of the advice.

'She's a busy bee,' Mum says. 'Always was.'

She gets up and starts to clear the table.

I help.

'Dad's anniversary is coming up,' she says, suddenly. 'Will you be around?'

'Of course. What'll we do? Same as last year?'

She nods. 'He never liked a fuss and you know what he thought of organized religion. So no ceremony.'

'Will James be over?'

'He's busy but he said he'd call.'

'OK, so it's just the two of us.'

She smiles and pats my hand.

'Are we rich, Mum?' Chloe asks as I tuck her into bed. We are so late it's not funny.

'Why d'you ask?' Keep it brief.

'Well, there's loads of money all over the house.'

Coins, unfortunately. 'We're not rich, honey. That's small money. You need lots of big money to be rich.'

'Oh.' She sounds disappointed.

'We're not rich. We're not poor. We're somewhere in the middle. We don't have to worry about money. That's the most important thing. Now go to sleep.' I ruffle her hair and kiss her forehead.

'You should go back to work. *Then* we'd be rich.' Maybe it was a mistake to tell her we couldn't get certain things because I've given up work.

'What's so great about being rich?' I ask.

'We'd have lots of money and we could buy anything.'

'Would you like me to go back to work?'

'What's this about rich?' Ian asks, swashbuckling into the bedroom after a hard day down the mines or financial equivalent.

'We're not rich, Dad.'

'Not yet.' He winks at Chloe then kisses her goodnight.

Sam is asleep. We cover him back up and kiss the top of his head.

I made an effort with dinner – roast chicken isn't actually that hard – and Ian seems to appreciate it.

'Let's get a babysitter,' I suggest.

He grimaces.

'Just for an hour. To go for a walk.'

'We need to cut back. We can't go on spending like we are.'

'I know. I've totally cut back but I need to get out. I've had the children all day.'

'Right, then, you go. I'll go later.'

'Who'll I talk to?'

'I'm serious, Kim. Once a week is enough for us to go out, for the moment – at least until I'm permanent. We've the mortgage to think about.'

No point suggesting a new kitchen then. I grab my keys and phone, briefly worry about axe murderers, then remind myself I'll become one if I don't get out.

'See you later then.'

'See you later.'

His kiss feels like a consolation prize.

eleven

After a day of tantrums (Sam), whining (Chloe) and total frustration (me), I do not greet my husband with a warm bosom, slippers or even the standard, 'How was your day?' What he gets is a flat, 'I'm going for a walk.'

He looks at me.

'It's either that or lose my mind. They're in bed.' I head for the door before he finds out Sam's still awake.

'But I'm just home,' he says, like another child.

'You're dinner's in the oven.'

'I was talking about your company.'

'I'll be great company – when I get back.'

There's a gentle thud from upstairs and then a succession of smaller ones. Sam appears at the top of the stairs. The demon child looks so suddenly adorable, all soft and squishy, hair defying gravity.

'Sam, back to bed.' I turn to Ian. 'Or you could have a man-to-man chat while you're eating dinner? I'll put him to bed when I get back. I won't be long. Promise.'

'All right, go on then.' He sighs and heads up the stairs to our son.

I try to ignore the permission-granted tone of voice and hurry into our neighbour's house for a pee. I can't risk going back – I might never get out again. I also borrow a hat. It's freezing. It's summer and it's freezing.

I walk fast, arms pumping. I even break into a run. It does help. By the time I get home, I'm feeling almost human. Ian is unconscious on the couch, his arm around our sleeping son. I take a moment to admire them, then slip Sam out and carry him up to bed.

I take out my laptop and try to fix *Peripheral Fear*, the novel that is proving a peripheral nightmare.

Friday and Connor is throwing a party.

'Guess who's babysitting tonight?' I ask Sam to distract him from the fact that I'm washing his hair.

'*Sally?!*'

'No, Sally wasn't free. Guess again.'

'Angela?'

'Got it in two, mister.' I turn to his sister. 'Chloe, I need you to be a little more careful about what you say to Angela, this time. No more talk about hairy arms.'

'I was just trying to help.'

'I know, sweetie, but you've got to trust that Angela can look after her own body, OK?'

Last time, Chloe suggested that Angela shave her arms because they were 'hairy like a man's'. By way of encouragement, she added that *I* always shave mine. When Angela suggested that I might shave *under* my arms, Chloe insisted, 'No, she shaves her arms.' The fact that Angela relayed the story in vivid detail gives me hope that she wasn't too upset by the unintentional hairy arms insult.

Angela arrives to a hero's welcome – from all three of us. I hurry upstairs to get ready.

I throw on the outfit I managed to select earlier. I stand in front of the mirror, something I haven't been doing much of, lately. Good God, are those my hips? I try different trousers. And look worse. I resort to black and promise to exercise.

In the bathroom, I put on make up, another forgotten activity. I squint and lean in to the mirror. Is that a *grey hair*? Jesus Christ. There's a full-length silver strand amongst the black. I literally run for the tweezers. I am thirty-three and *ageing*. Worse: I'm euphoric at the thought of a night out. What is happening to me?

Ian is in no rush to the party. He wants to go for a walk and have a quiet drink first. No argument from me. I, am, out.

'Any news?' he asks, as we stroll along the sea front.

I remind him of the hairy arms incident.

We laugh and I think that's all we need, time alone together. It's so good to be just the two of us that I don't care how late we are for the party.

When we do arrive, it's to a buzz. Connor introduces us to various couples already deep in conversation. He settles on 'Frances and Simon' who seem to be experiencing a chat-lull. We exchange 'heys'.

'Kim's a novelist,' Connor announces. 'The next Deirdre French, they say.'

I blush.

'Wow. That's great,' Frances says. 'What kind of novels?'

'It's just a hobby.' I turn to glare at Connor but already he's slipped away.

'Murder mystery,' Ian says with a confidence I don't feel.

'Wow! Gosh. I'd love to write.'

'You should,' I enthuse, diverting the focus to her.

'Ah, I'd never have time. I work full-time in the home. Our kids are very small.'

I nod, hoping that Ian is listening.

'Maybe if I got *some* support from this guy...' She points a thumb at her husband then leans in to me, conspiratorially. 'What *is* it about men? As soon as you become a full-time mum, they think they can treat you like a full-time slave.'

'Nice to meet you both,' Simon says and walks away.

Oh my God, the poor guy. He looks so hurt.

Frances rolls her eyes. 'Now *I'm* the bad guy.'

Ian and I exchange a glance.

'Look at him,' she continues. 'Guzzling away, assuming I'll drive home because I'm breast-feeding.'

Ian starts to move. I tighten my grip. He is *not* leaving me with her.

'*Now* I know why he encouraged me to breast-feed. Who has to get up in the middle of the night, every time? I'm living proof that sleep-deprivation is torture.'

Ian turns to me and squints. 'Isn't that Connor calling us over?'

It isn't. 'Think so, yeah. It was so lovely meeting you, Frances.'

'Oh sure, no problem.' She sounds disappointed. 'Good luck with the books.'

'Thank you.' The really worrying thing is that I feel her pain. Highway to the Danger Zone.

As soon as we're out of earshot, Ian stops and turns to me. 'Promise me you'll never turn into that.'

'Hey, thanks for the vote of confidence.'

'Sorry. It's just like my mother all over again. *Please* don't become a nag.'

'I'll do my best, Ian,' I say sarcastically.

'Sorry. She just freaked me out.' He takes a deep breath. 'Come on.' He links my arm like we're an old couple; this on the day I discovered a grey hair.

Before we can reach Connor, he jumps up on his coffee table and taps the side of his glass with a spoon.

The room falls silent.

'So, thank you all for coming. Great to see everyone I care

about here together in one room. Well, this is a going-away party, folks. I'm moving to London.'

'You haven't landed that MD job with Excell, have you?' calls a guy beside me.

Connor's smile says it all.

There's a round of applause and some whooping.

'So I'm standing up here like a tool to remind you all that I'll be under an hour away by plane. And I have a spare room. A big one. So...*come*!' He raises his glass. 'To continued friendship.'

'To continued friendship,' rises a united voice.

He steps down and is surrounded by well-wishers, mostly female.

Ian hands me his glass. 'Got to take a leak.'

I lower myself onto the arm of Connor's couch to digest the news. Friend Number Two down. Maybe I *should* think about tennis.

'Shove up,' Connor says.

I move along. 'I didn't even know you were job hunting!'

'I wasn't. I got head hunted. Poor fools have no idea what they're taking on!'

I laugh.

'Let's book your visit now.'

I give him a look.

'I'm serious.'

'Connor, I'm at home with two kids,' I say, feeling a bit Frances-y.

'Bring them. And Ian.'

I don't drag up the issue of money. Knowing Connor, he'd offer to pay.

'Sure I'll see you when you're in Dublin. I *assume* you won't forget us.'

He looks at me, serious suddenly. 'How could I?'

And I remember how close we once were.

twelve

I drive Mum to Kilcoole, a pebble beach at the foothills of the Wicklow Mountains. Mum and Dad first met here when Dad's football landed on her picnic rug. Five years ago, we followed Dad's last wishes and scattered his ashes here. If we wanted to visit him, he said, at least we'd get a trip to the sea. I was only glad that he opted for cremation. It meant that we finally got the cancer. Burned it to ashes, every last bit.

So here we are, sitting in silence on the very same picnic rug, looking out to sea.

'Remember the dolphins,' Mum says with a smile and I think she must be psychic.

I nod, smiling too. Dad stayed in the water while we shot out, fearing shark attack. The dolphins came right up to him and they swam together. He called us back in. And we went. Such was our trust in him. God, how I loved him, a bigger kid than us always, a total messer. I don't remember any of my friends' fathers being such fun.

'He was a great dad,' I say.

'He loved you both so much.'

'Wish he'd got to see Chloe and Sam.'

'He does see them, sweetheart. I'm sure of it. I know he was a stubborn man when it came to his lack of faith but I know he got through those gates somehow.' She smiles again, staring at the horizon. 'He had his own way of doing things, your Dad, his own way of looking at the world; but he was a good man, Kim, a good man.'

On the way back, we stop off at a little church. Dad might have had his own way of doing things, but Mum does too.

If anyone *ever* asks me for advice on writing (unlikely), this is what they'll get: Don't tell anyone that you're doing it. All you get is pressure. Sarah, on the line from Bangkok, has just asked if I've set myself a deadline.

'What kind of deadline?'

'You know – if you're not published by a certain date, you'll move on to something else.'

'No, Sarah, no deadline.'

'OK, change that.'

'Why?'

'It will keep you focused.'

'Right.'

'Well?' she asks.

'Well what?'

'Have you come up with one?'

'What, like now?'

'No time like the present.'

I bite my hand – rather than her head off.

'I'm waiting.'

'All right then! Two years! I'll give it two years. Happy?'

'Seems a little on the long side.'

'Call me patient. We can't all be an overnight success.'

'Did you get on to Jackie?' Jackie is acting editor at *Girlfriend*.

Sarah suggested to her that I write an opinion column for the magazine.

'She said she'd get back to me.'

'Let me call her, put a bit of fire under her ass.'

'Maybe don't. She might just resent me.'

'No. She'll resent me.' She laughs. 'OK, let's flick ahead two years. What'll you do if the novel doesn't work out?'

'I've two years to worry about that.'

'True. But it's always good to have a back-up plan. What's yours?'

I hate the way Plan B keeps popping up – especially as it's invalid – no money, no qualifications, no experience. 'Open an art gallery.'

'I can *see* that,' she says as if she can't see me as a novelist.

'Anyway, how's Bangkok?'

'I'd give it a two on the dick front.' She goes on to explain why, in sordid detail.

'How's Perfect Man?'

'I'm keeping him keen.'

'What, you're not talking to him?'

'No.'

'But...'

'I know what I'm doing.'

OK, that's a line I need to learn. I hear her pull on a cigarette. 'Wait. Are you back *smoking*?'

'I wasn't cut out to be good.'

I smile. 'So where to next?'

'Kenya. Then home, I think. I'm a bit shagged.'

'Literally.'

She laughs – deep and hoarse. 'Literally.'

'Bet you miss the rain,' I say, sarcastically.

'What I miss about home is the rain, the greenness...'

'...and the pint of Harp.'

'And the friends coming in...'

'And the pint of Harp...'

'And Sally O'Brien and the way she might look at you...'

'And the pint of Harp…'

'You could fry an egg on the stones here…'

'If you had an egg…'

'And you could certainly sink a pint of Harp…'

'If you had a pint of Harp.'

We laugh.

'I can't believe we remembered. That ad is ancient.'

'You had the easy lines,' she says. 'Right. I better go.'

'Good luck.' I suppress the mummy in me who wants to remind her to use condoms.

'Thanks, hon.'

And then I can't help it: 'Be careful out there.'

'I'll leave being careful to you.'

'Hilarious.'

'Joking. Ciao, hon.'

'Ciao yourself.'

I call Jackie in *Girlfriend* and a few of my old contacts. If I could land a column, it would give me a profile which would make me more attractive to publishers.

Turns out, no one wants a column by Kim Waters. Why? Because Kim Waters doesn't have a profile.

That settles it; *Peripheral Fear* is on official holidays. I need to do something about the kitchen before the kids break for the summer even if it's to just paint the cupboards.

'Any luck with the column?' Ian asks over dinner.

I shake my head, then explain.

'I can see their point. Who'd want to read about coffee mornings and cellulite?'

'*Excuse* me?'

'Joking.'

I raise my eyebrows. And fail to mention the break from writing. Normally, I tell him everything.

I start to clear up. 'Want to go to an art exhibition tomorrow? I'm going with Connor.'

He looks surprised. 'Who'll mind the kids?'

'I'm just going to let them here on their own.' Jesus. 'Mum will mind the kids, Ian. So, you coming?'

'What time?'

'Six.'

He shakes his head. 'Won't be finished.' Then he looks at me. 'Why are you going to such hassle getting into town for six?'

'It's not a hassle. It's the opposite. I never get out. Connor is moving to London next week. And the wine's free.' The last one's a joke to lighten the mood.

'OK.'

'OK? I don't need your permission, Ian.'

He looks at me like I've turned into Frances From The Party.

I am in love with a sculpture of an elongated, skinny man.

Connor, standing beside me says, 'It's good to have you all to myself.'

'It's good to *be* all by myself,' I reply without taking my eyes from my new love interest.

'You're not. I'm here.'

I laugh. 'You know what I mean. It's just good to get out.'

'I could be Quasimodo here and you'd still be happy – as long as you're *out*.'

'You know it.' I laugh. But it *is* good to be out on my own. Not as a mum. Or wife. Just me. Kim – the person who is becoming less familiar with every passing day.

'You love it, don't you?' he asks of the sculpture.

I nod. 'It's like a Modigliani.' I continue to gaze at it, trying to record every detail to memory.

'Buy it.'

I take out my phone and photograph it.

'What are you doing?'

'Buying it for free.'

'Buy it, Kim, for Christ sake.'

And I hate to sound like Frances but: 'I'm not working.'

'Ian is.'

'Yeah and I already hate relying on him for basic survival.'

'What about the bestsellers?'

'Bestsellers take time.' I take a deep breath and turn to him. 'Anyway, I'm taking a break.'

'What? From writing?'

'Just for the summer; don't tell Ian.'

He looks at me in surprise. 'Not like you to keep something from him.'

'I know. I know. I'll tell him. When the time's right.'

'Then let me buy it. A going-away pressie.'

'Connor, the idea of a going-away pressie is to give it to the person going away.'

'When have you ever known me to do anything the right way round?'

I look at him and smile. 'Thanks but no thanks. I'll buy it for myself – when I can.'

'It won't be here. It'll be in someone else's front room.'

I shrug.

'Right then, let me buy it for myself and when you're in the money you can buy it from me – if you still want it. How's that?'

I look at him hopefully. 'Seriously?'

He gives me an evil scientist look. 'I have ulterior motives.' He takes out his wallet. 'Come to London or you'll never see your little friend here again.'

I laugh. And hate that he's going just when we had begun to hang out again.

I have to lie down with Sam to get him off to sleep. He gazes across at me.

'What's you favwit twain? Pewcy or Thomas?'

I know what he's up to and press his nose. 'Sleep, mister.' I turn over or we'll be chatting all night.

He plays with my hair.

'Sam if you don't sleep, I'll go.'

Big sigh. ''K.'

I wake to the sound of Ian coming in. I check my watch – ten past ten. He gets later every day. I get up, grab a hoodie and go down.

'Hey,' I say, coming into the kitchen.

He turns around. 'Where were you?'

'Upstairs, lying down with Sam.'

'Well for some.'

'What do you mean?'

'Swanning around art galleries, napping whenever you want.'

'What are you talking about? I have the kids twenty-four-seven. Have you *any idea* how draining they can be?'

'They're good kids.'

'I know they're good. They're great. But they're kids. They demand, they fight, they whine. And they're a constant responsibility. You've only yourself to look after. You can come and go as you please, do what you want, when you want. Leave the office. Meet people for lunch. Buy things for yourself.' I look at yet another Brown Thomas bag he's arrived home with.

'Thought you said you weren't going to become a nag.'

'It's you that's becoming the nag, implying I've a great life and you don't. I don't have a great life. I've an OK life, like everyone else.'

'Yeah but you're doing what you want. And you're still complaining.'

'I'm *not* complaining. I'm defending myself – which I shouldn't have to do. You think you're the only person working around here and you're not. You're bloody not.'

'Have you been drinking?'

'I had a glass of wine. So?'

'You're drinking *and* minding children?'

'One glass of wine.'

'What's for dinner?'

'Nothing.'

'What d'you mean? What am I supposed to eat?'

'Whatever you want. You're a grown man. Work something out. Am I supposed to have something on the table for you every evening? Today I didn't get time. OK?'

'Right. I'm eating in the canteen in future.'

'You do that.'

'Right, I will.'

'Fine.'

'I'm going out.'

'Where?'

'McBloodyDonald's.'

I hope you choke, does not actually escape from my lips.

He slams the front door.

'Anyone home?' he asks an hour later, pulling back the duvet.

I'm under here, still trying to recover.

'What was that about?' he asks.

'I don't know,' I sniffle.

'I'm sorry. I don't know what got into me.' He sits on the side of the bed.

I sit up. 'Is everything OK at work?'

'Yeah.'

'You're not stressed or anything?'

He shakes his head.

'Sure?'

He nods.

'Because if something's bothering you, you should tell me.'

'Nothing's bothering me.'

'OK. Well, if anything does again, please don't take it out on me. I'm doing my best. I know I'm not an earth mother but I *am* trying.'

'I know. I'm sorry.'

'We shouldn't fight.'

'No. Come here.'

I scooch over to him.

He takes my hand and traces a finger over the back of it.

'Look, I know how hard you work especially with the book and everything.'

Oh crap.

'What?'

'Nothing.'

'What's up?'

I grimace. 'I think I might be suffering from writer's block.'

'Suffering?' An eyebrow rises.

'Yes, suffering. The harder I try, the worse it gets. I've tried changing the plot, the genre, starting over – twice. I'm going to leave it for a few weeks and try again.'

'Maybe you should speak to Sarah. She might have some advice.'

'I *have* spoken to her. She told me to write erotica.'

He laughs. And I feel like he's just told me I'm not sexy. Which I know is total paranoia.

'Kim, you've only just started. You don't want to stop now.'

'I want to settle into this whole mother thing.'

'What do you mean, "this whole mother thing"?'

'I want to be a good mum.'

'You are.'

'So why do you always make me feel I'm not?'

'I don't.'

'You do.'

'I think you're doing a great job with the kids. Sally's a hard act to follow.'

'Sally's not their mum.'

'Kim, I just said you're doing great.'

'Yeah.'

'About the writing, though… Aren't you afraid that if you stop you'll get out of the habit? You've never wanted to be just a housewife.'

'What's wrong with being "just a housewife"? My mother was "just a housewife" and my dad didn't have a problem with that. Would you have a problem with me being just a housewife?'

He hesitates. His, 'No,' is too quiet.

'You don't sound convinced.'

'Oh for God's sake, Kim. Do what you want. You do anyway.'

'What's that supposed to mean?'

'Nothing.'

'You didn't want me to quit work, did you?'

'Let's not talk about this now.' He's getting up.

'You didn't want me to quit and now you resent me for it. Why didn't you tell me you didn't want me to stop? I gave you enough chances.'

'I was happy for you to give up work. You had the novel. I'm just disappointed you're giving up on it so soon.'

'I haven't given up on it.'

'You quit work to write and now you're not.'

'For a few weeks.'

His sigh is dramatic. I look at him, really look at him. 'It's like your opinion of me is tied to what I do.'

'I just don't want you to become my mother. Or the woman at the party.'

'Thanks for the vote of confidence.'

'You've started nagging.'

'No I haven't.'

'You nag about emptying the dishwasher. Putting the bin out.'

'Dear Jesus, Ian, how do you live with me?'

'You see? There you go.'

'No. There *you* go.'

He sighs again and walks out. Minutes later, I hear the front door slam.

thirteen

'I'm taking up golf,' he says one Saturday morning. No discussion.

I look at him. 'Why?'

'I have to. They're all doing it.'

'Who's they all?'

'You know, people in the business.' I hate the way he says, 'in the business', as if he means, 'in the know', as if I'm not in the business or in the know.

'I thought you hated the idea of golf – the fact that it breaks up the weekend, takes you away from your family.'

'Yeah but this is important. You're not working now.'

My arms fold automatically and an eyebrow pops up.

'You know what I mean. I have to make this work, OK? I have to play ball.'

'There's a difference between "have to" and "want to".'

'All right then, if you insist, I want to. I want to play golf.' He walks around with both arms raised.

'Oh for God's sake, Ian. No one's under arrest here.'

He lowers his arms. 'I'm playing golf,' he says slowly, calmly. 'I'll be back by lunchtime.'

'Well, don't expect a pipe and slippers.'

He stares at me as though I've transformed into his mother.

Say nothing, say nothing. Count to ten. Count to one hundred. Don't, whatever you do, scream.

I take Chloe and Sam to the sea and try to forget as we search for shrimps in rocky pools.

'Dat's a puggle,' Sam says.

Do I explain that it is, in fact, a rock pool or teach him how to say puddle?

'Puddle, honey, puddle.'

'Puggle.'

'Puddle.'

'Puggle.'

'Say de, de, de, puddle.'

'De, de, de, puggle.'

I kiss the top of his head. Puggle it is. Side by side, we crouch, motionless, like three herons. Sam turns to me, reaches up his two chubby hands and places them on either side of my face and turns my head to him. He looks right into my eyes and says simply, 'My Mum' – just two words, less than 'I love you' but meaning more to me. My eyes smart and I laugh as camouflage.

'I see some! I see some shrimps!' Chloe says, pointing.

Sam picks up a stone and dive-bombs them.

My phone rings. It's Sarah wanting to know if I can meet her for lunch. She's home!

The minute Ian walks in the door, I walk out. I get the DART into town and find the trendy new restaurant that she's suggested and I've never been to. There was a time – not so long ago – I'd have been invited to the opening of any new venue in town.

She's at a table, whiskey in hand. She smiles that slow Jackie

Brown smile of hers, then stands and hugs me. She waits till I'm seated to ask:

'Jesus, Kim, what happened to you?'

I improve my posture and keep my jacket on. 'If you're talking about my weight, it's nothing I can't shift.'

'I was talking about your hair.'

My hand moves to it automatically. 'It needs a blow-dry.'

'Kim, that hair needs more than a blow-dry.' She reaches across and picks up a strand. 'It's full of split ends.'

I focus on the menu.

'And *what* are you wearing?'

'Something that fits.' It's meant to be a joke but comes out as a sad statement of fact.

She snaps open her designer bag.

'Membership card to my gym. Use it,' she says handing it to me.

I open my mouth to refuse but she holds up a hand. I take it to keep her quiet.

'Pop in any spare time you get,' is spoken like a person in a childfree zone, a place where nothing is ever broken or scribbled on and silence reigns, where one can hold a telephone conversation without interruption and have a pee in undisturbed peace on a dribble-free toilet seat. 'You're coming to Manuel with me tomorrow. No buts.'

'But...'

'*When* were you last at a hairdresser?'

'I didn't come here for a makeover, Sarah. There are mirrors in my house. I know, OK? I know.' And just like that I'm crying. In public.

'Oh God. I'm so sorry, Kim. I was just trying to help. This is all surface stuff, easily fixed. You're still beautiful. You're still a stunner.'

I blow my nose but the tears keep coming. 'I've stopped writing.'

'That's OK,' she soothes.

'I never see Ian. He's gone at half-seven and not back 'til nine or ten. All we do is fight.'

'He's probably under pressure in the job. Maybe he has a deal going down. You know how corporate finance is.'

'No, I don't know how corporate finance is and I don't care.'

She raises an eyebrow but says nothing. She passes me a fresh hankie.

'He used to bring Sam and Chloe swimming at the weekends. Not any more.'

'Probably exhausted.'

'He never does DIY. And there are so many things that need fixing.'

'Fuck DIY. Get a man in.'

'We can't afford a man. If we could, I'd be getting a new kitchen.'

'OK. Stop right there.'

'What?'

'Since *when* are you interested in kitchens?'

'Since I started spending most of my life in one. It's prehistoric. And dangerous. The cupboards are so crammed that opening them is a health hazard. A can of tuna nearly killed me yesterday.'

'Enough, about, kitchens.'

'At least things are good with the kids. I know them so much better now. I've time to listen, to understand that, usually, what they're asking or doing is just what I'd do if I were in their shoes.'

'Get back to Ian.'

'I don't know, Sarah. We've lost the balance. We used to be a team, both out working, both seeing equal amounts of the children, both independent. It wasn't perfect but we had loads of time alone together. We got on so well. Now it's all changed. He's the breadwinner – as he keeps reminding me. I depend on him and I don't want to. He's paranoid I'll turn into his mother. *I'm* paranoid I'll turn into his mother. We can't seem to talk any more. We argue all the time. There's nothing to laugh about. And we never,' I whisper, 'have sex.'

'OK. This is serious. A woman can't live without a shag.'

'Yes, a woman can live without a shag. Shagging is the *least* important thing. Just getting on, chatting, laughing, touching. They're the things I miss most.'

'Right. You need to get back working. And fast.'

'I didn't quit just to go back. I want a different life.'

'Don't you miss the buzz of work?'

'No. Not the buzz, not the endless meetings, not the impressing clients. None of it. Staying at home is hard; I'm an entertainer, barmaid, bum-wiper, cook, nurse, psychologist, teacher, cleaner, negotiator, fight-breaker-upper....'

'Stop, stop, for Christ's sake. No wonder he's never home – you're boring him to death. Will you for God's sake get a job, woman, before it's too late? You need your independence. You need to remember who *you* are. And you need to start fucking your husband.'

'Must be great to have all the answers, Sarah.'

She reaches across and grips my hand. 'I'm worried about you, Kim. You're going off the rails, hon.'

'You have *no idea* about my life. I gave up work for a reason. And if Ian doesn't like me as I am, screw him. I'm my own person. I won't be pushed around and made to feel less than I am.'

She bites her lip.

'Anyway. Enough about me. Let's order. And talk about you.' Her favourite subject.

'All right,' she says grudgingly. 'Just one thing – leopard-skin lingerie – never fails.'

Despite myself, I laugh.

So golf on Saturdays it is. And, what with his post-golf rest, he becomes *The Invisible Man*.

fourteen

A surprising thing happens. I grow to like his absences. His not being around means I can relax. Be myself. Do my own thing – well, *our* own thing; I still have the kids obviously. Weekends become a continuation of weekdays, just the three of us at our own pace. I suppress feelings that we should all be together and manage to succeed until confronted by scenes of happy families, especially tricky when they are people we know. Initially they ask where Ian is. Eventually they stop.

I develop a game. It's called, 'Who Loves You?' and it goes like this:

'Who loves you, Sammy?'

'Poo.'

'Who loves you, Samuel?'

'Poo, Poo.' He collapses into laughter. At least he has a sense of humour, however warped.

I have another go. 'Who,' tickle, 'loves,' tickle, 'you?'

'Mummy.'

'Yep and who else loves you?'

'Chlo.'

'And who else?'

'Dad.'

Mission accomplished but I keep going. 'And who else?'

'Gwanny Flowence.'

We go through all the grandparents, aunts, uncles, cousins, friends, even pets until I'm satisfied that they feel very, very loved.

One Saturday, I'm walking by the sea with two ice-cream-covered children. One of Dublin's most high profile, society couples zips by in their Mercedes Sports Convertible, top down. No sign of their peculiarly named children. At first, I envy them. Then I look down at Sam and Chloe and feel so much love. My kids are fun. More fun, now, than my husband.

'Can you iron this?' he asks. No, 'please'. No, 'would you mind?' No, 'whenever you get a chance'. To him, I am The Scrubber, Mrs Kavanagh. I wouldn't mind so much, if he'd show some appreciation. That's all I'm after. Acknowledgement. I *am* a person. I *do* exist.

The children aren't blind. Despite my games, they notice.

At bedtime, Sam asks the all-too-familiar question. 'Whay's my dad?'

'At work, sweetie.'

His head drops and he makes a muffled sound.

'How about a story? How about two?'

A car pulls up outside.

Sam jumps from the bed and races to the window, shouting, 'It's my dad! It's my dad!'

I glance out only to confirm what I suspected – it ain't him.

I ruffle Sam's hair and lift him up. 'He'll be home soon, sweetie. Would you like a *Winnie the Pooh* ice-cream?'

'Don't want ice-cweam, want my dad.' He starts to cry.

Not far behind, I take a deep breath. 'I'll tell you what; why don't we all stay up late tonight 'til Dad comes home? Wouldn't that be great?'

'Yaay!'

I set them up on the couch with a quilt and ice creams. I put on a DVD. 'Back in a sec,' I say lightly.

In the kitchen, I ring Ian to see if he can get home early or at least earlier than late. When he doesn't answer his mobile I try his direct line. A woman answers.

'I'm sorry. Mr Kavanagh is unavailable. Can I take a message?'

'Who's this?'

'His secretary, Melanie.'

Didn't know he had one. 'Could you ask him to call Kim as soon as he gets out, please?'

'Does he have your number?'

'He should. I'm his wife.' Ha, ha.

'Oh, Kim, hi! So good to talk to you! I'm Melanie. I just started here. I'm sure Ian's told you.'

Actually, no. 'Congratulations. And welcome to the firm.' A joke for myself. 'The firm,' has become one of Ian's favourite expressions. When he actually expresses.

'He's so great to work for,' she gushes.

Why is she telling me this? Does she want me to pass it on? 'When do you think he'll be free, Melanie?'

'He's in a meeting but he should be out soon. I'll get him to give you a call.'

'Thanks.'

He calls – to let me know he has another meeting.

'Until when?'

'I don't know. It could go on.'

'OK. Fine. But they're staying up till you get home. They need to see you.'

'Kim, they'll be exhausted.'

'I know. But they need to see you.'

He sighs. 'I'll do my best.'

Sam has fallen asleep on the couch by the time Ian gets home. Chloe is tired and cranky and more interested in the treats he has brought than in seeing him. Silently, I put them to bed. I wish him back to his old job. He mightn't have been happy but at least we saw him. And he wasn't Superman, just Ian. Approachable, fun, Ian.

'Sorry,' he says, when I come back downstairs.

'Why do you have to work so hard?'

'It's the business I'm in. Everyone around town's working this hard at the moment.'

Around town? Seriously? Any day now, he'll start using 'going forward.'

'Ian, I don't know much about corporate finance but do you really have to be busy all the time?'

'What can I do? I'm trying to make an impression. I thought you'd understand.'

'I do. At least I'm trying to but I'm beginning to wonder what's the point of working so hard if it means you're never around. What's life all about?'

'Have you been reading that crap again?'

'If you're referring to my self-help books, I got rid of them. But that's not what we're talking about here. We're talking about us growing apart as a family.'

'*Are* we?'

I look at him for a long time. 'Yes, Ian.'

'What do you want me to do?'

'Spend more time at home.'

'I can't.'

'Well maybe I could bring the kids to see you some lunchtime?' It would be worth wading through traffic for.

'I don't think so.'

'Why not?'

'I'm not always free.'

'I know but you must be sometimes. You could give us a ring.'

'No.'

'Don't you want to see us?'

'Oh for Christ's sake. I don't want you dragging yourselves into town to meet me for half-an-hour, OK?' He sounds like he's talking to a child.

'What about weekends? You could take them swimming again. They really miss that.'

'We'll see.'

The old chestnut parents have been trotting out for generations. I give up. What's the point?

He's not happy with the quality of the dry cleaning.

'So bring it back,' I suggest.

'Why didn't you check it?'

'Why didn't you bring it yourself in the first place?'

'I was busy.'

'As was I but I managed to do it – despite having two toddlers in tow. Couldn't you have held up the world of corporate finance for five minutes? I don't think it would have ground to a halt, do you?'

'I didn't think I was asking too much.'

'I didn't mind doing it, Ian. But if it's not up to scratch, you bring it back.'

He mutters something.

'What did you say?' I ask.

'It doesn't matter.'

'What did you *say*?'

Nothing, apparently.

'You know, Ian. If you're not happy, you can leave at any time. Any time.' Whoa, where did that come from?

'How about now? How does now suit?'

'Now suits just fine.'

My heart is pounding. We stand glaring at each other, neither wanting to back down, yet neither wanting to move forward either. How did an argument about dry cleaning turn into this?

Suddenly Sam is shouting, 'Leave my mummy alone.'

Jesus. When did he come into the kitchen? How much has he heard?

'It's OK sweetheart, Daddy was only joking.' I bend down and take him up into my arms. I look at Ian. 'Weren't you, Dad?'

'Yes, Sam, Daddy was only joking. I'm sorry if I upset you. I'm really sorry. Daddy loves Mummy. And Mummy loves Daddy.'

Then Sam does a wonderful thing. He rubs my back, round in circles, finishing off with a few gentle pats. 'OK, now?'

I nod and smile but I'm fighting tears. 'Thanks, Sammy. OK, now.' That's when I see Chloe standing inside the doorway, sucking her thumb. 'Hey, little lady,' I start but she turns and runs out. Still carrying Sam, I go after her.

I end up bringing them to McDonalds – the comfort zone of family.

Later, we sit in bed, reading, Ian *The Economist*, me an article claiming that parents who neglect themselves have poorer relationships with their children. I have counted twelve out of the twenty signs that show I'm in danger.

'Jesus,' I whisper.

'What?'

I pass him the magazine. 'This is me.'

He puts down *The Economist* and skims the article. 'That's not you at all.'

'It's not?'

'You don't take drugs.'

'Not yet! What about the other points?' I'm referring to such things as rushing around, doing several things at once, being repeatedly late, rarely saying 'no' to demands, having no time for self, having little or no leisure time or social outings, lacking exercise, being over-tired, rarely or never asking for help and, unfortunately, over-eating. 'You can't recognise me in that?' Maybe he genuinely doesn't know how I live.

'Well, they're me too.'

'*You?*'

'I do nothing but work.'

'You golf.'

'For work.'

'At least you get to be by yourself.'

'Maybe I'd *like* to see you. Maybe I'd *like* to see the kids. Did you ever think of that? Who wrote this shit anyway?' He slaps the magazine with the back of his hand. 'Psychologist! Should have known.' He throws it on the bed.

I turn over angrily and flick off my bedside light. I am the parking ticket on his windscreen; if he doesn't see me, I'm not there.

In the morning, we're getting dressed when I hit on a solution.

'Let's get an au pair.'

'An au pair? *Why?*'

'She could help with the kids and do light housework.'

'Haven't you time to do all that now that you've given up on the book?'

'I was thinking it might allow me to get *back* to the book.'

'Where would she stay?' He is finished knotting his tie but still looking at himself in the mirror.

'We could put her in Sam's room and move the kids in together.'

'But you did it up for him. He loves it now.' He's baring his teeth at himself, checking them out.

'Sam and Chloe like sharing. You've always said so.'

'What about our privacy? Having someone around all the time. I'd hate it.' Now he's squinting at himself.

'Our quality of life would be better, though. We could go out for a walk in the evenings.'

'What about sex? You don't think we could have sex with a stranger in the house.'

What sex? 'We could try it for a while and see how we get on.'

'Not interested.' He drags himself away from his reflection.

It's official; the earner has become the decision-maker.

fifteen

An invitation arrives for Ian and, quelle surprise, his family. It's a barbecue organized by his 'firm'. On the plus side: it's a day out together. But there is also this: I will spend my time chasing children while Ian talks business with work colleagues. And this: The women will probably be gorgeous.

'I think I'll give it a skip,' I say to him when he arrives home from work.

'You can't.' He shoots me a look.

'Why not?'

'Because it's a family day.' He thinks for a second then adds, 'and they know I've a family.'

I laugh. It's like he already considered the option of pretending we don't exist. 'You could say I was sick or something.'

'Why don't you want to go?'

Hmmm. Do I want to point out that I'm now a size fourteen and no longer in the workforce? 'I dunno.'

'Ah, come on. It'll be great. Dave's bringing his family. You'd love his wife, Emily.'

I don't know Dave. What makes Ian think I'd like his wife? 'Does she work?'

'No.'

Ah, my answer, right there. Neither of us works therefore we will get on famously.

'Please come, Kim. You're always saying we don't spend enough time together.'

It's his first offer of time with us. I can't throw it back in his face. 'OK, I'll go.'

'Great! What'll you wear?'

'What?'

'Just wondering what you'll wear.'

'Why?' Is he afraid I'll turn up in a shiny tracksuit and a pair of Sarah's shoes? I'd have to buy a tracksuit. But I could. It'd be worth it just to see his face.

'I'm trying to have a conversation. Isn't that what you wanted? Jesus.'

'Did I ask you what you'd be wearing?'

'No but I'm happy to tell you. I'm wearing my chinos, this shirt and the navy rugby top thrown over my shoulders.'

I laugh. Then realise he's serious.

'What's so funny?'

'Nothing. I thought you were joking. You don't usually plan your wardrobe.'

'I'm still new – or at least I still feel it.'

'The chinos would be perfect,' is my apology.

'Can you wash and iron them for me? I'd like them to be fresh.'

That's it. Where are the Golden Pages? I'm getting a new husband.

Barbecue Day dawns sunny. A sign, I hope. I have adopted the cunning use of posture and loose clothing. Sam and Chloe look respectable. Ian is immaculate. His recently commenced early morning jogs are paying off. Maybe Sarah is right. Maybe he is my sexy husband.

We arrive at Fitzwilliam Square on time. Ian introduces me to a few of his colleagues, then his boss. She reminds me of my ex-client, Maeve, not just in appearance but demeanor. Ice, basically. Superior Ice. Which sounds like a decent brand of vodka.

I'm glad when the formalities are over, though Ian, as expected, leaves me with the children. It's a challenge keeping them out of trouble, what with the ready availability of raw meat and things to knock over, including themselves, the barbecue, other children, their father's work colleagues and catering staff carrying hot food. I divert them to the bouncy castle and stand guard, ready for rescue.

And then I see her. She is every man's dream – a blonde Betty Boop. But forget dreams – what's she doing all over my husband? Touching his arm, whispering in his ear, hanging on his every wonderful word. If Ian notices, he doesn't let on, chatting casually to people I don't know. Every so often she throws back her blonde head and laughs – with her whole body. I try to invoke calm. Breathe in blue, breathe out orange (advice of sadly-missed colour therapy book). I grip my sparkling water.

Ian glances over and when he catches me looking gives me an encouraging it'll-all-be-over-soon smile. She follows his eyes and sees me. Lock on. I have never worried about other women; I will *not* start now. I turn back to the bouncy castle where life just couldn't get any better. I can't help it though: I glance back. Oh my God, she's on her way over. I find myself pushing up my sleeves.

'Kim?' she breathes. She offers her hand, 'I'm Melanie. We spoke on the phone?'

'I remember,' I say coldly. I also remember she was working late.

'Ian's such a great guyyyy. It's so great working for him.'

'Great.' What can I say?

'You're so luckyyy.'

'I am?'

She throws back that beautiful head as she laughs.

'And what do youuu do? You're at home, right?'

'Actually, I write. Fiction,' I say, hoping she won't ask if I've a publisher, an agent or even a basic plot.

'From hooome?'

'Yup.'

She looks into the bouncy castle. 'Which ones are yours?'

I point them out.

'Sooo cute.'

'You like children?'

'Oh my God. I so love them.'

'Maybe you'd like to mind mine for a while?'

She looks at me, unsure for the first time. Then she laughs but nervously. The suggestion gets rid of her. Off she totters, her excuse being an empty glass.

He never told me she was attractive. Correction. He never told me she existed.

I'm standing at the bathroom door, leaning against the frame. Ian is cutting his toenails into the toilet.

'So when did you get a secretary?'

'Melanie?' He looks up casually. And I can't tell if it's too casually. 'We took her on a few weeks ago. Didn't I tell you?'

'No. You didn't.'

'Yeah, well. Things have been hectic.'

'I know.'

He turns and his voice softens. 'There's a big deal going through, should be finished soon.'

'Maybe you could take a few days off.'

'Yeah, maybe,' he says uncertainly. 'There'll be a lot to tie up.'

'As long as they're not people.'

'What?'

'A joke, honey. A joke.'

'Oh.'

'She fancies you, you know.'

'Who? Melanie? Does she?' Altar boy innocence.

'You know she does.'

'OK so maybe she has a little crush. It's harmless. Anyway, you *know* how I am with other women.'

And that's why I never worry. I've always thought him overcautious, keeping a professional distance from the various child minders and babysitters we've had. Now I'm reassured. When I think about it, he hadn't been encouraging Melanie. He hadn't even been looking at her. He could have shaken her off though; he hates people clinging to him. But maybe she's good for his image – a pretty, attentive secretary, hanging on his every word. Where would a pirate be without his parrot, a soldier without his stripes, a corporate financier without his secretary?

'Look, I'm sorry I haven't been spending more time at home. I'll make it up to you. I promise.'

'The kids' summer concert is coming up,' I say hopefully.

He grimaces. 'When?'

'Last Friday in June.'

He makes a face. 'I won't make it, hon.'

Suddenly I'm close to tears. For once, he seems to notice. He takes me in his arms, something he hasn't done in ages. But something's different. It's like he's appeasing a child.

Connor calls and my smile is automatic.

'There's a man over here *pining* for Ireland. Come and *save* him.'

'Pining as in: not eating, not sleeping, not functioning pining?'

'Exactly.'

'Aren't there any nice London girls to cheer him up?'

'Only you will do. He's just not the same without you. He looked so happy leaving the art gallery...'

'*Who* looked so happy leaving the art gallery?'

'Modigliani man.'

'Connor, are you trying to tell me that a piece of stone wants me in London?'

'Well, I could also do with some serious slagging.'

'How about some telephone slagging?'

'Not the same. Sorry.'

'Not sure how I can help then; I can't come over with the entire posse.'

'Course you can.'

'I wouldn't be able to give you my full slagging attention.'

'That might not be a bad thing. Come on, Kim. It'd be great to see you all. I'm so bored.'

'How's the job?'

'Job's actually good. Challenging. And I've found an amazing apartment. Loads of room. Could fit a family.'

I smile. 'You're not going to give up, are you?'

'Great art galleries over here.'

I sigh.

'And parks for the kids. And restaurants.'

Maybe I should stop fighting this. 'Let me see how much the flights cost. No promises.'

'Excellent!'

sixteen

Sarah calls from New York City.

'The search is off. I've found him – Perfect Man.'

'I thought you already had.'

'Seems there are degrees of perfect.'

'So who is *this* guy?'

'An artist. Sculptor, specifically.'

'Wow.' I'm thinking Leonardo, Michelangelo, Picasso.

'Name's Theo…'

He's even got the 'o'.

'It's true what they say about youth,' she says, dreamily.

'How young is he?' I ask cautiously.

'Twenty-three…'

Actual relief. Over the age of consent. I'd worried that the research might have sent her over the edge.

'He's *so* hot, Kim.'

I could definitely be more interested. 'Yeah?'

'Not a million miles from Ian, actually.'

'Describe him.'

'Pink and orange hair. Totally fit. Hung like a horse.'

'Just like Ian.' Sometimes there is no understanding her thought process. 'How did you two meet?'

'I answered an ad for an artist's model.'

I imagine what it must be like, hanging out with an artist in New York City. 'So, has he taken you to the Met?'

'No.'

'Museum of Modern Art?'

'No.'

'The *Guggenheim*?'

'No.'

'Then what are you doing?'

'Use your imagination,' she says, huskily. 'Anyway, just rang to say I'm coming home. My publisher wants me to start my promotional tour in Dublin. Seems I'll be all over the media. Every paper you pick up, there I'll be, grinning back at you.'

Scary. 'And what about Theo?'

'Oh, Theo's coming. I'm his muse. And he's mine. It's the perfect relationship.'

'Relationship; that's new.'

She sighs dreamily. 'I know. I've never felt like this before.'

'Wow. That's great. I'm so happy for you.' I think back to when I first met Ian. We had that, then. All of it. Now it feels like I'm remembering two people I barely know.

Ian doesn't make the children's concert. Mum makes up for his absence with positive energy and cheery smiles. I hide my disappointment. There are other absent dads of course. But they probably never make these things. Ian used to. Always.

The children are bewitching. Sam has roles as a doctor, a prince and the sun. Chloe is typecast as a frog. But such a cute frog. I'm incredibly proud and struggle to record them and still witness some of the fun without a lens separating us. And yes, I *am* one of those mums. It's either look ridiculous or trust the scene to memory and I've invested too much to have it forgotten.

Post-concert, we go on a Treat Picnic. It's meant to consist of nothing but treats, some healthy (dried apricots, juice and popcorn) and some not (Skittles, Rancheros, wine gums and Curly Wurlys) but Mum breaks the rules and brings along some home-made scones. I forgive her when I taste them. We keep fruit pastilles for Ian – his favourites – or at least they used to be. I'm not sure of anything about my husband any more. The children make us laugh and I log this memory, instinct telling me I might need it.

Like a squirrel, I've started to store the good times. Sam climbing rocks singing, 'We will, we will wok you'. Chloe telling me that dogs 'drizzle'. Sam tottering around in my forgotten high heels with his trousers at half-mast. The kids asleep, still and floppy, small, pale and vulnerable. Hugs. Kisses. Cuddles. Little legs running. Little hands tickling. Brief moments captured in time – shrimp hunts, pillow fights, dressing up, rolling down slopes, eating bread meant for ducks, being given weeds – memories I've begun to stockpile as clouds gather on the horizon.

I spend the summer making Jacuzzis (take a children's paddling pool, add washing up liquid and warm water), building sandcastles, applying sunscreen, witnessing growth spurts, discovering the endless potential of the simple handkerchief and learning the basics of first aid. But the hardest thing is trying to come up with answers for things I don't understand. Like why planes crash if a window breaks. Why some animals are meat-eaters while others won't touch the stuff. Why the sun never burns out. And why their dad is never home.

Deirdre French keeps popping up everywhere. On the radio – receiving the Woman of the Year Award for her contribution to literature. In the newspaper – topping the bestsellers list. Her success is a glaring reminder of all the two thousand words I've let fall between the keys, of the plots that stank and the characters that never came to life.

In the evening, when I could be writing, I spend what's left of my energy trying to interest Ian in the comings and goings of family life. It proves a bad investment. I witness him lose all semblance of interest in us, not even bothering to pretend any more. I get used to putting three plates on the table and remembering not to call him for meals.

When he *is* home I often wish he weren't.

'You never wear your black trouser suit any more,' he says with audible regret.

I know my clothes have taken on a heavy animation influence but: 'You want me to wear a suit around the house now?'

'No.'

'When then?'

'I don't know, maybe when we go out.'

'When *do* we go out?' Now that Angela has left to see the world and Sally has moved to Cork.

'In theory.'

'You want me to wear a suit when we theoretically go out?'

'I don't know.'

I could call Sarah in frustration. But I know what would happen. She'd ask if I'm wearing leopard-skin lingerie. And she's a feminist.

So I do it. Buy the lingerie. Get my hair cut. Subject myself to some serious waxing. I even squeeze into the black trouser suit and lie in wait. Nine o'clock comes and goes. The killer knickers are riding up my bum. Ten o'clock and I'm beginning to wonder how big an idiot I am when, finally, in he walks.

'What's for dinner?' are his first words. Not, you'll notice, 'you look stunning', 'love the hair' or 'get naked now'.

I clear my throat, then, in an attempt at sultry, I look down at the suit.

Blank. Totally blank.

I give up. 'Pasta.'

'With that sauce you're always buying?'

'With that sauce I'm always buying.'

'Oh.'

He sits at the kitchen table expecting to be served.

I land it down in front of him. I run upstairs and rip off the suit. I fire those sexy ass-cutters in the bin. The under-wired bra gets mangled and meets the same fate. I drag on my old reliables: comfortable PJs, socks and hoodie. I flop onto the bed, beginning to feel my toes again, beginning to feel myself again. Is there anything as unsexy as a desperate woman? Oh yes, an available one. Before, I had a reason to dress up: work. Now I've none. And if it's not good enough for him he can shag bloody well off.

The helpful suggestions keep coming. I should take more exercise. Have I thought of using colour in my hair? Someone in work lost a stone at Weight Watchers. Almost to spite him, I dress down, eat up and watch my ass finally give in to gravity. Eventually, I get sense and just ignore him. He does the same to me.

When I buy a very essential tumble dryer without checking the bank balance, he takes to muttering, conducting little tête-à-têtes with himself for minor offences like the way I make dinner, hang the clothes on the line, walk, eat, breathe, live. I'm not perfect. But I never was. And he didn't seem to mind before.

Bed has become a popular hiding place. He uses it. I use it. At separate times, obviously to avoid seeing, hearing, smelling, touching or, heaven forbid, tasting each other. Our conversations, such as they are, revolve around mortgages, bills, schools and repairs. Plenty of flat monosyllables involved. Enough to make me want to scream just for variety. What-do-you-thinks and how-do-you-feels are part of our past. We have become lodgers, sharing accommodation but not our lives. Gone are calls from the office to see how I am. I'm no longer on his agenda, except when he wants me to do something. Angela has gone to see the world. There are days I want to do the same.

seventeen

One evening, to get away, I call over to Mum's.

'So, how is everything?' she asks, pretending not to be surprised to see me at this time. She folds away *The Irish Times* crossword. Out comes the carrot cake and on goes the kettle.

'Fine. How're things with you?'

'I was going to ring you actually. I've a little bit of news.'

'Oh?'

'Well, it's nothing really...'

Which means it's something.

She clears her throat. 'You know Charles Bradshaw – my solicitor?'

'Yeah?'

'Well, we've actually been out on a... date or two. I hope you don't mind.'

'Why would I mind?' Outside of the fact that Charles Bradshaw is a total plonker and she deserves better.

'You know that no one will ever replace your father, Kim.'

'I know, Mum.'

'And a woman can get lonely...'

Don't I know it? 'If anyone deserves some fun, it's you.'

'Charlie is good company.'

'*Oooh*! "*Charlie*" already? You don't hang around.'

'Stop.' She slaps my arm. 'You're terrible.' But I can tell she's delighted.

'Do I detect a little blush?'

'I'm a bit long in the tooth for blushing. Charlie has been very kind, that's all.'

'Can't fool me. I know looove when I see it.'

'He's a good listener. And it's only been three early birds.'

'Mum, stop trying to defend yourself. Just enjoy it. I'm really happy for you.'

She smiles in relief. 'Thanks, love. I just thought I should mention it. Just so you know.'

'Well, carry on,' I say in my best Sergeant Major accent.

The kettle boils and she gets up to make the tea.

While her back is turned, I innocently say: 'I never saw you and Dad fight but you must have sometimes, right?'

'Of course we had our arguments. Everyone does, don't they?'

'But were there bad patches, you know, times when maybe you didn't talk to each other?'

She turns and eyes me carefully.

'Just wondering,' I add.

She carries the tea to the table but forgets to pour, too busy looking at me.

'All marriages go through bad patches. It's hard when two people are together all the time, especially with the demands of children. But I think that no matter what, you have to try and keep the lines of communication open. Never let the sun go down on an argument.'

'That's a cliché.'

'There's truth in every cliché. Kim, if you're worried about something, talk it through.'

Oh crap. Here come the tears.

'Aw, love. What is it?'

I shrug not trusting myself to speak or it'll all come tumbling out.

'Why don't I babysit at the weekend? Let you and Ian out for a chat.'

I shake my head. I can picture it now, staring across some irrelevant meal with nothing to say to each other, like those sad couples you see and want to cheer up.

'How about next Friday night? Whatever this is don't let it simmer. Nip it in the bud.'

I sigh deeply.

'I've just bought *The Aristocats* movie for the children. I'd love an excuse to watch it with them.'

'What about you and Charles?'

'Honey, I think Charlie can survive a night without me. This is the man you love.'

Right now I don't feel very loving towards him. But this is our marriage. I have to do something to save it. So I nod. 'Thanks Mum.'

Friday arrives and, though I'm dreading the evening, I take such care getting ready. Then, I sit well outside the splatter zone while the kids eat their dinner.

'Dis basketti is scwumptious,' says Sam, sucking up a long string of spaghetti.

Lovely to hear a) my favourite word, basketti and b) someone compliment my food.

But actually, they're *so slow.*

'Come on guys, Granny'll be here soon.'

'Can I be finished?' Chloe asks.

'Two more spoonfuls.'

She gobbles them down. And jumps from the table.

'Me too?' Sam asks.

'All right.' They won't die of starvation.

Mum arrives looking gorgeous. Must be love.

I take the DART into town and walk to Ian's office.

I have to wait at reception for fifteen minutes before he appears. But he looks incredibly handsome and I smile, not quite believing that this man is married to me. What is happening to me?

We go to Guilbaud's. And I'm not sure that that doesn't reek of desperation.

Small talk isn't happening. I see him look at my hands and realise I'm fidgeting.

'Ian? Can we talk?'

He loosens his tie, clears his throat. 'Yeah, sure.'

'Do you think we're getting on?'

He hesitates. 'Do you?'

I smile. 'I asked you first.'

His return smile is stiff. 'It's been tricky since you gave up work. You've become…' He pauses. 'Sensitive.'

'What d'you mean?' Keep calm. Breathe.

'I feel I can't say anything or you'll bite my head off.'

Don't bite his head off. 'Anything else?'

'Well, we're not having fun any more, are we?'

Don't sound accusatory. 'Why do you think that is?'

'Well, you seem a bit down since giving up work.'

'*I* seem down? You're the one it's bothering.'

'*What*?'

'I'm just not good enough for you any more. Am I?'

'What are you talking about?'

'Maybe I am a bit sensitive. Maybe I am a bit down. Did you ever think of asking why? There's the fact that you're never home. There's the fact that when you are, you give the distinct impression that you'd rather not be. And there's the *fact* that I'm trying my bloody best.'

I cover my face. Tears were not on the agenda. Neither was blame. Once again, I've screwed up.

And still, it could turn around. This man could reach out to this woman. He could hold her hand and tell her what she needs to hear. That he loves her. Still admires her. That she's good looking, has a great ass, is a super mum and that he's sorry he's been busy but he'll try to be around more and that he finds his family fascinating, *fascinating* human beings.

Does this happen?

No.

The bill arrives.

With perfect timing, the credit card machine malfunctions and Ian is asked to sign the old fashioned way. He digs his signature in, tearing through the entire thing. The waiter practically sprints from the table. Ian stands suddenly and strides off as if he can't get away from me fast enough. I follow at my own pace, clinging to my posture like it's all I have left.

eighteen

It's sausages that convince me to go to London. It happens like this: Sam and Chloe place an order of rashers and sausages with the Kitchens. While I'm at it, I ask Ian if he wants anything. Three sausages, comes his exact reply.

'How many did you do for me?' he asks when I place one in front of him.

'Three.'

'Where are the other two?'

I look at him. 'Cooking,' I say, rather than, 'up my sleeve'.

'I wanted them at the same time.'

'Are you *serious*?' I don't include the word 'fucking' – there are children present.

'Mu..uu..um,' whines Sam. 'You neva got me a fowk.'

I roll my eyes and retrieve the desired utensil. 'You know, sometimes I feel like moving to a desert island inhabited only by women.'

'Can I come?' asks Chloe enthusiastically.

'Yes, honey, you can.' I kiss the top of her head.

Then I decide. London will be my desert island.

I wait till that evening to tell Ian.

'Why?' he asks sitting on the bed, unbuttoning his shirt.

'You'll be off at that conference anyway. And I need a break.'

'Can't you wait till I get back and we'll all go on a weekend away together?'

As if that would *ever* happen. 'That'd be great. But I'm also going to London. You won't be here to miss us. I may as well.'

'But why do you have to go and see Connor?' He's standing now, facing me.

'He's the only one inviting us. And I'm not spending money on a hotel. I thought you'd be glad. The flights are so cheap.'

'Don't you think it's a bit iffy going off to stay with another man?'

I laugh. 'We're talking about Connor here, not some sex God.'

'What about his drink problem?'

'Connor doesn't drink.'

'Yeah but we all know what happens when he does.'

'That was a long time ago. He hasn't touched the stuff since. It's not as if he's an alcoholic. Drink just doesn't suit him.'

'He has the hots for you, you know.'

'What?!' Now who's paranoid?

'Maybe you don't notice but I do.'

'You just don't want me to go.'

'No. I don't. He has a history of violence.'

'When he drinks. Which he doesn't.'

'I don't want you to bring my kids over there.'

All of a sudden they're *his* kids. As for his opinion of Connor... 'You know, Connor sees you as a friend.'

'OK, let's not fool ourselves here. Connor is your friend. I tolerate him.'

Jesus. 'Big of you.'

'Why do we always have to fight?' He drags on a T-shirt and walks into the bathroom.

I follow. 'On this occasion because I stand up for my friends. And for the record, that is what Connor is. A friend. He doesn't fancy me. I'm not his type.'

He turns from the sink, toothbrush in hand. He does a deliberate head-to-toe sweep of me, then says, 'I suppose you're right,' as if he means, 'you wouldn't be anyone's type.'

'I'm going. With or without your approval.'

'Sure, go ahead, what do I care?' He flings his toothbrush into the sink as if he cares very much and then sighs, his millionth this month.

I lie in bed, seething. My friendship with Connor goes back to school. Whatever relationships we were in, we always stayed friends, best friends. But you can't be best friends with a guy when you're married. I gave up our closeness for Ian. And now he pulls this. Drink isn't a problem and he knows it. *Once* Connor reacted badly to it. Some eejit started moving in on his girlfriend. Connor lost it. The guy ended up in hospital. Connor got sorted with a psychologist, stopped drinking. End of story. End of problem. It should *not* be used against him. I'm sorry I ever told Ian. But then I tell him everything. Or at least I used to.

The days pass with mounting excitement. Sam because he'll be going on the Underground; Chloe because she'll be going on a plane; and me because I am: a) getting away b) seeing Connor c) going to London and d) not coming back. OK d)'s a joke. For now, I'm off and feeling a little giddy.

Ian calls from work wondering what time we're flying out on Friday. Apparently, he'd like to see us off. Why the sudden interest? I'm available round the clock.

'Actually, we're going on Thursday.'

'Thursday? I thought you said the weekend?'

'Long weekend. The flights are less expensive that way. We leave Thursday, back Sunday night.'

'OK. Whatever.'

I soften. 'Ian, you won't be home anyway. And we'll all be in better form when we see each other again. I know we will.'

'Gotta go here.'

'OK. Off you go.'

'Off you go,' he says unhappily.

In Arrivals, Connor breaks into a smile and waves exaggeratedly.

I laugh. 'Eejit.'

Physical contact (his simple hug) is a recipe for tears. But I am strong. I am a warrior.

'It's so good to see you!' he says. Not: 'God, you look terrible,' or any of the wide variety of ass comments he could make, like: 'What happened to your ass?' or 'I see you've brought your ass,' or 'How did you get THAT through Customs?' He just whirls us away.

Driving through London in his open-top, I begin to feel human.

His pad in Chelsea is minimalist chic. Modigliani man fits right in.

Oh my God. He's gone out and bought a little wooden train for Sam, a fairy outfit for Chloe and a miniature painting for me.

'Jesus, Connor.'

'Didn't want you guys to be bored here in the bachelor pad.'

He pours me a glass of wine, instructs me to sit down and puts a coffee-table book on Art Deco into my hands. Then he transforms into a horse and plays with my kids. I am so grateful to let someone else take over for a while.

When they are, finally, tucked up in Connor's gigantic spare bed, (Chloe still wearing her new fairy outfit and Sam holding his train), Connor makes cocktails. His is non-alcoholic. Mine is a Cosmopolitan. He holds out a frosted glass housing an icy pink drink and it feels like I'm on holidays.

'Cheers!' he says. 'Dinner in a sec.'

'Connor! We can get takeaway!'

'I've everything ready to go. Was busy chopping while you were putting the kids to bed. Anyway it's just stir-fry.'

'Want a hand?'

'I cook alone.'

Thank God, I think, closing my eyes and tilting my head back. I take a deep breath and exhale slowly. Then I take another sip. Watching Connor clatter around the kitchen brings me back to a time when a young economist, trying to impress his new girlfriend, cooked her a meal. Out of tune and using the wooden spoon as a mike, he sang, 'Climb every woman.' He wasn't trying to be funny; just didn't know the lyrics. And that was it, the exact moment I fell in love.

I don't know when I last heard Ian sing or look as carefree as Connor does now. Last time I saw him laugh was at the barbeque. My heart sinks as I realise the truth: he is happier at work than at home. I knock back what is fast becoming Cosmo-medicine.

nineteen

We remember old times, good times, ridiculous times. Ridiculous people. Great people. I laugh to the point of pain. And my heart soars. Because I am still me. After all.

Over coffee I go quiet, remembering how things are at home. I look at Connor and decide that now would be a good time to save him. Because something good has to come from my mistakes.

'Con, I want to tell you something important, something *really* important. Are you listening? Because this's really important.' OK, I'm drunk.

He smiles. 'I'm all ears.'

I point at him. 'When you get married, make sure it's to the right woman. Live with her first – for, like, seven years. Or more.'

He raises his eyebrows.

'I'm serious.'

'You and Ian didn't hang around, though, and you're happy.'

I shake my head sadly. 'No. Not any more.' My sigh is like all the sighs in the world combined.

'But you're like, I don't know, Dempsey and Makepeace, Fred and Wilma....'

'Maybe we *were* Fred and Wilma. But Fred changed when Wilma quit work. Wait, why are we talking about Fred and Wilma?'

'How has he changed?'

'Oh, I don't know.' I wave an impatient hand. 'Doesn't matter. This isn't about Ian. It's about you. Don't rush, OK? Take your time. Be *sure*. You know?'

'OK but what's up with you guys?'

'Nothing. It's OK. We'll sort it out.'

'Only that we made a pact, remember? If one of us is in trouble, the other's there.'

'We were twenty-one.'

'So?'

I shrug. I feel so suddenly tired.

'Hey,' he says so softly. 'What's up? It can't be that bad.'

From where I'm sitting, it couldn't be worse. 'He doesn't love me any more.' There, I've said it.

'I'm sure that's not true.'

'He's changed. Ever since I quit work, he's lost all respect for me – and he used to have a lot. Remember?'

'Your biggest fan.'

'Well, now he's never home. He's even taken up golf. It's like he doesn't want to be with us. It's like he thinks we're boring or suburban or something.'

'Go on.'

'The other day, the look he gave me for not hanging the clothes out properly on the line.'

'*What?!*'

Another sigh, equally deep. 'I'd been using the tumble dryer a lot so I decided to cut down on electricity, you know, to save money. I didn't think to clean the line before hanging out the clothes and, because I hadn't been using it, they got marks on them. I had to take them all down and wash them again. The look he gave me – like I'm the world's biggest moron.'

'Maybe you were imagining it.'

'I know Ian. And I know when he's being a bastard. He was being a bastard.'

'Maybe he was just being stupid. Maybe it didn't mean anything.'

I shake my head. 'He constantly finds fault with what I do, especially the way I look after the kids. If they're cranky, it's because I didn't make sure they slept enough. If they won't sleep it's because I let them nap during the day. If they don't eat, it's because I gave them treats. If they get sick, it's because I didn't give them vitamins. Everything, *everything*, is my fault.' I will not cry. I will *not* cry.

'All since you gave up the business?'

I nod. 'Maybe he only likes independent women or something. But I *am* working. I'm writing. Well, I'm supposed to be. That is, I will be after the summer. Anyway, minding two children is a full-time job. It really is.'

'Have you spoken to him about it?'

'We end up fighting. I'm doing my best. I'm trying to be a good mum. I'm trying to stay strong, confident but it's getting harder and harder. He's turned nasty.'

His eyes widen. 'He hasn't *hit* you?'

'No! *God* no.'

'Because I'd kill him. You *know* I'd kill him.'

'He wouldn't.' I shake my head adamantly. 'Whatever else, he'd never hit me.' Then I smile. 'I'd kill him!'

'At least you haven't lost your sense of humour.'

'No, I have. And I've lost my energy. And very soon, the will to save my marriage.'

'Surely, it can't be just because you gave up work? I mean, you're still the same person.'

'Try telling *him* that.' Then it strikes me. 'You know, because of all this, I'm becoming a different person: defensive and paranoid and depressed and sad. Are depressed and sad the same thing? I've never had a problem with confidence. Now, I feel this small.' I pinch the air. 'If I weren't a fighter, I'd be this size.' I close my finger and thumb so that they all but meet. 'I don't want to fight. And I don't want the kids to grow up witnessing that. But sometimes I'm just so frustrated I forget they're there. Sam shouts, "shut up, shut up," and covers his ears. Chloe goes really quiet. It's terrible.' My fingers dig into my forehead. My jaw jerks out of kilter; my lip wobbles and I'm crying. 'I'm sorry. I'm just so tired. If it wasn't for the kids I'd probably stop trying.'

'Shh,' he soothes. 'It's OK. We'll sort this out.'

I'm so glad of that 'we'.

He runs his hand over his mouth. 'What about counselling?'

'Ian wouldn't see a counsellor even if he had a hot stock tip – well actually, in that case….' But it's not funny.

'I'm sure he wants to sort things out too, though.'

'He thinks everything's my fault.'

'Maybe advice from a third party might mean something to him?'

'If he'd go.'

'I don't think you've anything to lose by trying?'

'Except another argument.'

'One argument versus saving your marriage...'

'I know you're right. I'm just tired of being the one doing all the trying.'

He just looks at me.

I take a deep breath. 'OK. I'll do it. I'll try and get him to go.'

He winks. 'Atta girl.'

I wake to shrieks of, 'Surprise!'

Connor carries my favourite breakfast in on a tray: toasted bagel, orange juice and coffee. Sam has the newspaper. And, from behind her back, Chloe produces tulips.

I touch my heart. 'Aw, you guys. Come here and give me a hug.'

Sam and Chloe race over, climb on the bed and snuggle into me.

I look at Connor. 'Thank you,' I whisper.

I check my watch – almost eleven. I haven't slept this late since I worked, back when we took turns to get up with the kids.

'Chloe was telling me she can swing all by herself,' Connor says. 'So, I thought we'd take the *Underground* to Hyde Park.' He looks at Sam as he says Underground.

Sam hops off the bed and bursts to the door. 'Let's go. Let's go.' He's jumping up and down.

'Hang on. I have to get dressed.'

'You're not coming,' Connor says. 'We're meeting you for lunch. I've written down the details. And you have my number.'

The *thought* of a morning to myself... 'You *sure*?'

'See you later. Come on, Chloe.'

'Wow. You really are a star.'

'As are you – you just have to remind yourself a bit, OK?'

I lounge over breakfast, take my time with the newspaper, delay in the shower – without one interruption, one request, one emergency. This is what heaven must be like, I think, as the water pounds down on me. I circle my shoulders, tip my head back and let out a long breath. Leaving the apartment, I feel as though I've washed away years.

I wander through art gallery after art gallery. My heart expands. My steps lighten.

And then I realise the time.

I rush into the restaurant, late, carrying a small oil painting.

'I am *so* sorry, Connor.'

He smiles. 'Just show me the painting.'

Excitedly, I unwrap it.

'What is it?' Chloe asks, frowning.

'A painting.'

'I know *that*. What *is* it?'

'Oh. Eh. I don't know. It's called abstract.'

They pass it around.

'So it's a picture of nothing?' Chloe asks.

'Pretty much.'

She nods. 'I like it.'

'Me too,' says Sam.

I notice a woman at a nearby table smiling at us. She looks at us and sees a happy family. And that floors me all over again.

As we're leaving, Connor tells me that his sister Grace has offered to babysit tonight.

'Wow, that's so nice of her.'

'She's devoted to... my money. She can come for half-seven. That OK?'

'Sure. I'll have the kids in bed.'

'Awww, Mum.'

'I'll read you a story first, of course.'

'Could Connor?'

I turn to him.

He looks at the kids. 'Connor could.'

'You're better than any shrink,' I quietly tell him.

'What's a shrink?' Sam asks.

'Someone small,' Chloe explains knowledgeably.

Another chic restaurant. Another window table. I join Connor in drinking Coke – easy to be thoughtful when it's no longer every woman for herself. Suddenly, I don't want to go home. I want to hide away here, burrow my head into sand. Instead, I raise my chin and determine to 'fake it till I make it'.

Too soon, we're at the airport and I'm fighting those ostrich feelings again.

'Thanks, Connor. So much.'

'Anytime. I mean that. Anytime. I'm here, OK?'

I nod.

'You're a bright, intelligent, beautiful woman. Remember that. OK?'

Why is it that when people are nice to you, it makes you want to cry? I force a smile. 'You've been amazing, Connor. You *may* even have restored my faith in men.'

'Steady.' He smiles. Then he scoops up the children.

I get a sudden urge to do what Chloe is doing: throw my arms round his neck and cling to him. And he must sense this because, once she's safely back down, he quietly says:

'Don't forget how strong you are, Kimmy. Sort this out. Find a counsellor. Make it work. For everyone's sake.' He looks down at Chloe and Sam and winks.

'Come on, Mum or we'll miss the plane,' Chloe says.

'I'll call you,' Connor promises.

Walking towards Security, I feel like a child on a Sunday night, dreading school next day.

twenty

Sunday night. Watching Ian drop his bags in the kitchen without a hug reminds me of the status quo. It also reminds me that he didn't call us while we were in London. He looks at me, sitting at the table going through Friday's uninteresting post.

'You look well,' he says accusingly.

'Thank you.' Nothing's going to get me down.

'How's Connor?' he asks walking over to put on the kettle.

'Well.'

'What did you do?'

I brighten, surprised that we're having an actual conversation. 'Just hung out mostly. On Saturday, he brought the kids to the park to give me a break, which was lovely.'

He turns. 'You let him take the kids out on his own?'

'Of course. He's great with them. They love him.'

'I can't *believe* you left him alone with the children.'

'Stop, OK? This is Connor you're talking about. Even if it

wasn't, do you really think I'd let Sam and Chloe go off with someone I didn't trust? Do you really think I'm that careless?'

He shrugs, the implication being that I am. Maybe he should check their gums. They've probably got scurvy. I am mortified and furious – mortified for myself and somehow Ian, and furious because he is accusing our (sorry, my) friend, the friend who looked after us so well, of being the worst thing in the entire world.

'Don't ever and I mean, ever, accuse me of not looking after the children properly. As for Connor, he was more a father to them this weekend than you've been in a long time.'

'Excuse me?' His head juts out.

'You heard me. If you'd seen the trouble he went to, the thought he put in, the time he spent with Sam and Chloe, you wouldn't be in such a hurry to knock him.'

He's walking towards me now. He reaches one of the kitchen chairs and grips the back of it. 'So, good old Connor was a great father. What kind of husband was he?' Nasty, nasty tone of voice.

I stare at him. 'You can just fuck off.' I walk out and slam the door.

In the bedroom, I simmer. And pace. When I finally seek him out it's because somebody has to fight for this marriage.

He's in the garden. Goose-stepping across the lawn.

'Ian, I'm sorry. You *are* a good father.' I don't add, 'when you're here', though I think it's a relevant point.

I get a look, nothing more.

'It's just that you were implying that I can't look after the kids and that's not fair. And your remarks about Connor were out of line. You know that.'

'*Do* I?'

'Yes you do. Connor is one of my oldest friends. He was, and always is, a perfect gentleman.'

He raises an eyebrow.

And I suddenly think: he's getting off on this, the power of it

– of me asking forgiveness and him deciding whether or not to give it.

'We need to see someone, someone who won't care who is right or wrong...'

'What, a shrink?'

'A therapist...'

'I'm not telling anyone our business.'

'We need to do *something*.'

'You know what I think of those people.'

'We can't keep going on like this. We need help.'

'How about you making more of an effort? That'd help.'

'So it's all my fault?'

'Why can't you be nicer to me?'

'Why can't *you* be nicer to *me*?'

'It's hard to be nice with you skiving off to London.'

'Skiving! I had two children with me. It was a weekend. You weren't even here.'

'I was *working*.'

'Can we please go to counselling?'

'Not interested.' He turns and goes inside.

I kick the swings – more than once.

Out front, I hear his car start up and reverse out – fast.

'Great; that will really solve things, Ian.'

I go inside.

Nothing like fury to get the housework done. I clatter around the kitchen in rage and frustration. He is winning and I am losing some secret battle he is waging and I don't even understand.

I stare out the window of a sparkling kitchen. Two robins are having sex on the swings. They might as well – someone in this house should be.

He doesn't come home. And I don't sleep.

The following morning, Connor calls. I close my eyes and

take a deep breath. I shouldn't have to do this, reverse out of our friendship because of a jealous husband. But I don't know what else to do. Things are just so bad.

'So, how did it go?' he asks. 'Did you arrange to see someone?'

My throat burns and my eyes smart. 'It's OK, Connor. We talked. We'll probably go on a holiday or something.'

'Oh. Good. But no counselling?'

'No.' Tears well over. I cover my mouth so no sound escapes.

'How are Chloe and Sam?'

'Good,' I choke.

'Such great kids. You'll have to bring them over again soon.'

'Mm hmm.'

'Are you *OK*?'

'Yeah,' I say lightly.

'What's up?'

'Nothing. Distracted.'

'By what?' he asks like he doesn't believe me.

'Writing,' I lie. But actually, it's what I should be doing – escaping in my mind at least, and reclaiming my independence.

'Oh Kim, that's great! Did you find a plot?'

I start to think out loud. 'I'm not going to worry about plot…or anything. I'm just going to see what comes.' My lie is becoming the truth. I'm going to do this. I have to.

'I should leave you to it.'

'Thanks, Connor.' Once again, he has rescued me.

'Call anytime you need to, anytime you want to talk.'

'Will do,' I lie.

'Do!' he orders.

'And listen, don't feel you need to call. I'll be fine. *We'll* be fine. Honestly. We just needed to talk.'

There's a pause. 'I might just touch base once a week or so.'

'Oh. OK. Sure. Would before seven be OK… just in case you wake the kids?'

'Of course. Talk soon. And Kim?'

'Yeah?'

'I'm so glad it's working out.'

'Thanks, Connor. For everything.'

In the notebook that my husband once gave me, I write about a woman who is losing herself, disappearing in the day to day.

Every entry records her growing isolation. The walls of her world move in on her a fraction more every day. She wonders if she screamed would anyone hear. She stops caring – not just about her husband but about everything. Other people's lives are moving ahead. Her new sister-in-law is pregnant. Her friend has got engaged to her latest Perfect Man. Her former child minder is starting college. She is becalmed. And no longer cares.

Her husband works later and later. She does not come downstairs to welcome home his disappointment. When he finally makes it to the bedroom, she pretends to be asleep. It's easier.

One night, he doesn't come home at all. She is surprised that, next day, he bothers to explain about the big deal 'going down', how he'd to work till two and how, because he had to be up at six, 'all the guys' stayed in the Conrad.

She wishes him back in his boring old job with his pre-*Wolf-of-Wall-Street* vocabulary. She wishes their old life back.

The children start to creep into her bed. She doesn't bother moving them out. He sleeps in their son's bed – when he *is* actually home.

twenty-one

Sarah arrives home with a penname – Sexton. Her debut novel is already a number one bestseller. *The Sunday Independent* wants an outdoor photo of the author. Sarah suggests my garden, thinking that she can catch up with me at the same time. Unfortunately, she fails to run this by me. So I don't get to warn her about the state of our garden.

Seeing it now, she realises her mistake.

'Jesus, Kim, what happened here?'

I glance at the kids, one of whom is watering the grass with sand.

'Here, grab the bike and scooters and we'll throw them in the shed.'

'What about all the other stuff?'

'That too. Guys, give us a hand. Everything into the shed.'

They jump up, excited at the idea of a sudden mission.

'Even the sandpit?' asks Chloe.

Sarah goes over. 'Good God. Is that muck in there?'

'We'll just cover it,' I answer them both.

'Aww, Mum,' complains a muddy Sam.

Sarah's look is: I-will-*never*-have-children. She checks her watch. 'Oh God.'

'Movie time,' I say.

'But we don't want a movie now.'

'I'll give you ice cream.'

They nod, coolly, negotiation complete.

Settling them in front of the TV, I glance out into the garden and smile. The manicured, coiffed, professionally-styled glamour puss is picking up mucky trucks with the tip of her finger and thumb and holding them out from her as she totters in her Miu Miu's to the shed.

Garden surprisingly respectable, we open a bottle of wine and wait for the photographer.

'So. How's Theo?' I ask.

She grimaces.

'What?' I ask.

She gulps wine as though washing down a pill. Then she sighs. 'That didn't work out.'

'But you were engaged!'

She lights up, takes a phenomenal drag, tilts her head back and blows smoke into the already grey sky.

'I'm so sorry,' I say.

She waves her hand. 'Lucky escape, really. Mummy fixation.' She tops up our glasses and raises hers. 'To the Irish male – seems you can't beat him after all.' But I can tell that she's gutted. 'How are things with you and that sexy husband of yours?'

I can think of a lot of adjectives; sexy isn't one of them. 'Fine.' Moving right along…. 'So how's fame?'

She shakes her head. 'Hilarious. Everyone wants to know who the real people are behind the characters.'

'I'm dying to read it.'

From her oversized designer bag she produces a copy.

'Wow! It looks great. Such an *achievement*, Sarah. Seriously. *Huge* congratulations.'

'Open it.'

It's autographed. Which is weird. Like I'm a fan. Which I'm sure I will be.... 'Thanks, Sarah.' I leaf through the pages, then glance up. 'You must be so proud.'

'Haven't really stopped to think. But yeah. I guess.'

'What's it like?'

'Well, it's a contemporary story of an affair,' she begins like she's surprised I haven't heard.

'No, I mean, the life. What's it like being a published author?'

'Oh, right. Yeah, fine. I guess. A bit weird total strangers coming up and telling you you've written their life.'

'Seriously?'

'Had a woman this morning. Told me she was just like the main character, missing the most obvious signs that her husband was having an affair. She didn't want to see it. Kept making excuses for him. When it was so *obvious*.'

'Poor thing.'

'Bit of an idiot, though. It was a textbook case. Late nights, always out, never up for a shag, touchy.'

Suddenly, this has become personal. 'People work late, Sarah. They get too tired to shag. Marriage is *hard*. Bloody hard.'

She stares at me.

'You don't know what it's like with kids. You just don't know.'

'Yeah and I don't want to.'

'You should listen to yourself sometimes. You sound so bloody smug, like you've life sussed and everyone else is a moron. Life is messy, Sarah.'

'Life with kids certainly is.'

'Yeah, well, be careful not to air that view in the media. There are people out there going through this shit. And it's not easy.'

'Point taken,' she says pointing her cigarette at me. 'Don't want to turn off potential readers. You always were good at PR.'

I look at her and wonder if she lost her heart somewhere between New Zealand and New York.

The doorbell rings. She takes out a mirror while I go let the photographer in.

'Kim? Kim Waters?'

'Hey, Pete!'

'What are you doing here?'

'I live here.'

'I'd *heard* you'd quit. Good for you. You're writing now, yeah?'

'Trying.' I smile.

I show him out the back and introduce him to Sarah. Then leave them to it.

I go in to the kids and tell them that our garden will be famous – we'll buy *The Sunday Independent* and celebrate.

Sarah stays in town for three days. On her last night, she calls around to say goodbye. Ian, who was never a fan, seems to find her suddenly fascinating, asking question after question about publishing. How did she find her agent? What's her fan mail like? Will her advance allow her to write full-time? And though I'm a shadow in the room, it *is* good to see him animated. And it *is* good to learn more about my dream world and have a new energy in the house. I know that everything about Sarah highlights my shortcomings. Still, her visit serves as a temporary blip in a downward spiral. I wish I could make it last. Instead, I call Connor and ask him to put her up. London's her next stop and she's tired of hotels. I hang up and immediately wonder if that was wise.

twenty-two

It's a Saturday morning and my birthday. Ian is up early, getting ready for golf. I go into the en suite to use the loo. He's standing in front of the mirror, slapping on aftershave.

I stare at him. 'What are you *doing*?'

He practically drops the bottle. 'What do you mean?'

'You're allergic!'

'Oh. This stuff's OK.' He lifts up the bottle.

'Why are you wearing aftershave all of a sudden?'

'I don't know. A change.' He checks his watch. 'Gotta go.'

I don't know whether he's forgotten my birthday or decided not to bother. I'm so used to not caring, I'm surprised how close to tears I come.

I bring the laptop to bed. And lose myself in words.

'Happy Birthday, Mum!'

I look up to see Chloe carrying in a tray, Sam skipping beside her. He gives a little jump. My heart lifts and breaks at the same time.

Their breakfast is Cornflakes mixed with Coco-Pops, soggy now and drowning in sugar.

'Thank you *so much*, guys. I'm so proud of you. Come up here beside me.'

'Eat up,' Chloe says.

'Yes sir.' I wink. And get going.

Beside me, they watch each spoonful reach its intended destination.

'Best breakfast ever,' I say.

We plan the day. Then kick it off with flying. Chloe goes first. I lie on my back, place my feet under her hips, my hands under her shoulders. She stretches out her arms and legs as I move her back and forward through the clouds.

'Wee,' we say together.

'My turn! My turn!' shouts Sam.

Finally, we go downstairs. Ian's golf clubs are lying against the back door. In his hurry to get out, he must have forgotten them. I'm surprised he hasn't rung to give out because, for some reason, this, too, will be my fault.

But he doesn't ring.

I remember the aftershave. And remind myself that I trust my husband.

The beautiful oil painting Mum presents me with makes me cry. Connor calls from London to send his best wishes. Then he puts Sarah on the line. They sound so happy, so carefree. So much younger than me – though neither is.

I bring the kids on a train ride. We have a picnic and feed the ducks on St Stephen's Green. And I try not to think that Ian should be here.

From the kitchen window I nurse a coffee watching them play in the sandpit, Chloe sifting sand like a domestic goddess. The gene must have skipped a generation.

Ian comes home smiling. He even gives me a hug.

I think, he's remembered.

'It's OK. I've eaten,' he says.

'How was the golf?' I manage.

'Great.'

'Didn't miss the clubs then?'

'What?'

'You forgot your clubs. I was surprised you didn't ring for them.'

His expression changes quickly but I see it in slow motion. Panic, embarrassment, guilt.

'I borrowed James's,' he hurries.

'James? My *brother*?' But how? James is in the States.

'No, James from work, the guy I play with.'

'Oh. You never mentioned him before.'

'Yes, I have. You just never listen.'

I would if he actually talked. He wouldn't have mentioned a James any more than he'd have mentioned a Melanie.

'So who is he?'

'Why the sudden interest?'

'You accused me of not listening; well, now I am. Who is he?'

'Just some guy at work.'

'Where does he live?'

'Malahide.'

'Malahide? And he comes all the way over here to play golf?'

'Golfers travel for their sport,' he says like he's in the know and I'm not.

'Where do you even play?' I can't believe I don't know where he goes on Saturdays. Don't I care enough to ask?

'Elm Park.'

'Really? I thought the waiting list was closed.' Thank you, morning radio.

'It is but the guys at work are members and got me in.'

'How much did it cost?'

'A few hundred.'

'Really, is that all?' He's actually lying to my face.

'I can't remember. It might have been more.'

'It's just that I thought we were checking big expenditures with each other.' Rule made after the tumble-dryer fiasco.

'Kim I happen to be earning the money around here.'

'So you keep reminding me.'

'So have we finished with the fifty questions?'

'No. We've only just started. Who is she, Ian?'

He narrows his eyes. 'What did you say?'

'You heard me. Who is she?'

'What are you on about?'

'I mightn't have tits the size of melons but I'm not stupid.'

'Well you sound pretty stupid, right now. For crying out loud. Do you *know* what you've just implied? Do you have *any idea* how that makes me feel?'

I smile rather than puke. 'Don't ever take up poker, Ian. You're a shit bluffer.'

'What are you talking about?'

'Attack has always been your chosen form of defence.'

He looks stunned.

'And for the record, I don't give a *shit* how you feel. Your clubs are under the stairs. And the children are in the garden. Mind them for a change.' I walk out.

I run upstairs, heart pounding. There is no golf, no James. And the aftershave? Camouflage. To remove the scent of her. And maybe I knew that this morning. But I trusted him – or needed to. I grab a pillow and fling it at the wall. He's right. I *am* stupid. How long has this been going on? I have to know. Everything. Though it will kill me.

The desperate hunt for receipts begins. Receipts for what, though? Lingerie? Romantic meals? Chocolates? Spa treatments? Movies I haven't seen (i.e. anything non-animated)? Where does he keep them? He doesn't do the accounts at the kitchen table any more – that, in itself, is suspicious. Where does he do them, now?

And where does he hide the receipts? I throw my hands in the air. Who am I? Jessica Fletcher? And why Jessica Bloody Fletcher? Why not Temperance from *Bones*? Or some other gorgeous creature.

Maybe he keeps them in the attic.

I can't search, not properly. Not while he's in the house.

I hear Sam and Chloe on the stairs. Sam calls me. Can't Ian do that one thing – just keep an eye on them while I implode? I hurry into the bathroom and splash cold water on my face.

'What are you doing up here?' Chloe asks.

I turn off the tap and scrub my face with a towel. I look at her and smile. 'What are *you* doing up here? I thought Dad was minding you.'

'He's cross.'

I sigh. 'OK.'

I bring them back down. And the only reason they stay is because I put on *Monsters Inc.* and give them ice cream.

'I'll be down soon,' I tell them.

At the end of the stairs, I see his briefcase, tucked behind the coat stand. I don't bother to check if the coast is clear, just grab the black rectangle and run upstairs. In the bathroom, I lower the lid on the toilet seat. I sit staring at the combination lock. I used to know the magic numbers – my birth date. It used to be in all his passwords. I hold my breath and move the dials. The snap pops open and I'm filled with despair. He hasn't even tried to hide this.

I sit looking at the interior of the briefcase, unable to take the next step. You see, I know this briefcase. I bought it. We joked about the secret compartment. If he has used it to hide his dirty secret, it will be the final blow.

And yet I can't sit here forever.

I take a deep breath. And open it.

My heart is pounding, my palms sweaty. Part of me wants to know. The other part chooses denial.

The strong part wins.

I reach for the compartment.

twenty-three

Eight hundred euro for two nights in Rathsallagh House Hotel, a nice, cosy remote spot. I check the dates against my calendar. Working in London, supposedly. Sneaky, slimy, sniveling...shit. But there's more. Meals at Mao, Guilbaud's – and Bang (appropriately enough). But these are public places. And Guilbaud's is *our* place. I feel my heart rip open.

We've been so generous with our joint account. We've bought her a trip to a spa. We've funded outings to the National Concert Hall and the Gaiety Theatre. All the things I've been missing while he's been nagging me to cut back. I know what *I'd* like to cut. Why couldn't he have done any of this with me? She gets all this for what, a little acting, a little pretending he's fantastic? Maybe she really believes he is. Try living with him; try being his *wife*. No picnic, I can tell you – whoever you are. But I know who you are. It couldn't be more obvious.

How long has it been going on? When did it start? Did she

move in on him or he on her? Does anyone suspect? They must. It's probably the office joke. Six days a week he sees her. Saturday mornings and nine-to-five. More. Do they both 'work late' every day? Or do they go somewhere? Her place? Where *is* her place? My money is on Malahide, home of the invented James. Has Ian moved in an extra toothbrush, razors and, let's not forget, aftershave? Does he complain to her when he has to go home?

Does he love her?

I throw the briefcase and its grubby secret at the wall, loosening plaster and sending receipts, documents and a random apple flying. I leave it all behind me, racing downstairs and grabbing the keys from the hall table. I'm gone.

A sunny Saturday afternoon and all the happy families are out. I leave suburbia. Fast. I hit the open road and press my foot to the floor. Has he told her yet that I know? Will she be relieved? Will she tell him that now is the perfect time to leave? The cliché, the secretary. I could find her number – so easily. I could ring and hang up. Give *her* something to worry about. Become a psycho. Plead insanity if caught.

My phone rings. I ignore it. At last, it stops. Almost immediately, it starts up again. This happens over and over until finally, I reach for it. His face is up on the screen. This man I loved. I want to fling the phone from the car. Instead, I put it on silent.

What do they talk about? Sex? Me? Does he tell her he doesn't love me, that he's only staying because of the children, that he's planning to leave, that it's only a matter of time? Does he mean it? How does she make him happy? I'd like to know because I've been married to him for seven years and, clearly, I can't. Is she good in bed? Is she an animal? Insatiable? Does she have multiple orgasms? What are her wildest fantasies? Come to think of it, what are his? What's she like naked? Does she have a tattoo, birthmark, extra toe? Does she have cellulite? Even a little? Does she insist on condoms? She'd better. Does she have a brain? But then does she need one? Grey matter might get in the way. Does he have a pet name for her and vice versa? I want to know everything. And nothing. Were *any* of those late evenings at the office real? He knows, obviously, but I don't.

Only when I find myself driving into Wexford town do I wake up to how long I've been on the road. I've done a two-hour drive in one-and-a-half. I pull over. Take stock. Or try to. All I know is I'm not going back.

I drive to the only hotel I know in Wexford. We stayed here once just before Sam was born. I was an entrepreneur then and could afford four stars.

The receptionist swipes our credit card – our credit card for three.

'Actually, why don't you make it a suite, please? Go crazy.'

'Certainly.' She smiles as if to say, 'I like your style.'

In the suite, door closed behind me, I do something I never do. I open the mini bar.

I raise a miniature bottle of gin to the sky. 'Cheers, Ian. You prick.'

I knock back a gin and tonic, then go rock star and throw the tiny, plastic bottle at the wall.

I run a bath. I fill it to the top with scalding water and bubbles. I lie, soaking, trying to block out thoughts. But they invade my head like a mistress does a marriage.

What am I going to do? I can't stay here forever. There has to be a solution. I see Sam and Chloe's faces in my mind. Innocent. Soft. Round-eyed. I wail into my hands. I take deep breaths. Try to calm down. *Think.*

What do I want? Just focus on that. What, do, I, want?

Outside of murder, I don't know. I don't know what I want.

One thing's for sure, there's no going back.

And maybe I don't fucking want to.

Despite a constant assault on the mini bar, my mind won't

stop. I want him out. Gone. But can I do that to Chloe and Sam, make their Dad go away? I could give him an ultimatum – she goes or I go. But I'm going nowhere; *he's* the one who's going. If he's going. Maybe he'll leave anyway. Maybe he's been planning to all along. Wow, the hurt of that. Did he wash their teeth? Did he remember to put a nappy on Sam? And. What am I going to do?

The morning sun pierces my eyes. I sigh deeply and get up.

I feel the psychological pull back to the kids.

But they are with him.

What do I do?

I start with a full-Irish breakfast and have it served on the balcony. I inhale the briny sea air and watch the sun spark off the sea.

Maybe I should never have got married. Stayed like Sarah. But…the kids.

I go down to the beach.

I pelt stones, one by one, at the breaking waves, but really at him. Did he sleep? The fucker.

Stone after stone. After stone.

Screeching children run into the sea beside me. I cease fire, turn and wake to the world around me. Children fill moats with water. Two fight over a bucket. A boy pees on the sand. A crying girl stands over an upturned ice cream. Beyond the chaos, a woman lies on a sun lounger, reading. An oasis of cool, she reminds me of Sarah. Calmly, she turns a page.

Sarah. What would she do? The answer comes instantly. She'd tell him to leave. But Sarah doesn't know the responsibility of keeping a child's world safe, secure, steady. They need their father. But. They've needed him for quite a while now and he's been off enjoying himself elsewhere. What kind of father would they actually lose? And what kind of mother would I be if I allowed them to witness me lose all respect for myself – because that is what will happen if I do anything other than tell him to go.

twenty-four

I can't confront him until the children are in bed. Fine! Let him have them for the day and see that it *is* work. I arrange a late checkout and buy a swimsuit in the fitness centre. I return to the beach where I swim out past the waves. I turn and pound through the water, parallel to the shore. Suddenly, I'm swimming and crying, gulping air and water. I struggle towards the beach and, when my feet reach sand, I stand, coughing and gasping.

Recovering, I see my sad little pile of clothes on the beach and wonder what would happen if a current took me. They'd find the clothes and think I'd given up. A roar rises inside me. I will not give up. I will not lie down. I will not roll over.

I have lunch, a full-body massage and a haircut. I buy an amazing red dress in a boutique attached to the hotel. It's five when I – reluctantly – leave. I would like to say that I'm all fired up – in chest-beating mode. But I am ending my marriage. Leaving the man I've loved. Sending my children's father away.

So, actually, there's only one word for the way I feel: sick.

Their curtains are closed. My heart aches. Can I do this?

I have to.

I take a deep breath and go inside.

'Skip your teeth,' comes Ian's voice from the landing.

Sam cheers.

'I *want* to do my teeth,' Chloe insists.

And I think: Go, Chloe.

'All right, hurry up,' Ian snaps.

'Whey's my mum?' Sam asks.

Suddenly, I want them down here in my arms. I want to wrap them up, protect them from this. Instead I'm going to hurt them.

'She'll be home soon,' Ian says.

Oh yeah?

'Come here, little man. Let me put your nappy on.'

That he remembered the nappy seems such a big thing. When it shouldn't be. Oh, God. Here come the tears. I hurry into the kitchen where I try to get a grip. But the pitter-patter of their little feet upstairs sends me over the edge and I escape to the garden. I gulp air. Tell myself I can do this. I have to.

'Kim?'

I turn. The relief in his eyes almost melts me. But then I think of them together.

'Hi,' is the feeler he puts out.

'Hello, Ian.'

'Where were you?'

'Does it matter?'

He looks so sad. Good.

'How are you?' he asks.

I stare at him. 'Really? *Really?*'

'We've finished that deal.' His voice is hopeful.

'What deal?'

'The Eirplay deal that had me working so late for so long. The big buy-out everyone's talking about. It's all over the papers. Surely I told you about it?'

'No, Ian. You didn't.' I sound tired. I *am* tired.

'Anyway, I just wanted to tell you, I won't be spending so much time at the office. I'm taking a few days off, a week off and I've just booked flights to Rome.'

'For who? You and me or you and her?'

The colour seems to drain from his entire body. 'I'm not going to deny it.'

'It's not like you can – *any more.*'

'I've too much respect for you to....'

'You know nothing about respect, you...you *shit.*'

'Kim. Listen to me,' he says softly, coming to me.

'Don't come near me.' I glare hatred.

He stops, takes a step back.

He may be shocked but nowhere as shocked as I am. It's been confirmed. Those few simple words, 'I'm not going to deny it', have killed any tiny hope that there might have been some mad, crazy explanation for those receipts. I walk past him, into the kitchen because the break up of this marriage is not a spectator sport.

He follows me inside. 'Kim, you have to listen to me.'

'I don't have to do anything.'

'We have to talk.'

'Really?'

'For the sake of the children, please.'

'*Don't* use the children.' And then I'm imagining their little faces. 'How could you do it to them? They're too small for this. Too innocent. How do I tell them? How do I explain? No, hang on, *you* explain. You explain it to the children. And while you're at it maybe you could let me in on a secret. Why? Why did you do it, Ian? Wasn't I good enough for you, exciting enough? Didn't I boost your ego enough? Is that it?'

'Kim. I'm sorry.' He starts towards me again.

'Stop! If you value your life, you won't take another step.'

He stops. 'It meant nothing. I love you and the children more than anything in the world. I'm sorry…'

'That I found out?'

'It's over. I'm going to move job.'

'I don't care. I don't want you near me. I can't even look at you. Get out. Just get out of my life.'

'No.'

I stare at him.

'It's over with her,' he insists.

'You expect me to believe a word you say? I don't know when this started. I don't know what was a lie or what was the truth. *You* know but I don't. Do you think that's fair?'

'No,' he says, voice hoarse.

'So, go,' I say, so terrifyingly calmly.

'Don't do this. Don't block me out.' So he knows me after all. He knows how I am if people mess me around. I snap the shutters down. Forget their existence.

'Kim, you have to listen to me. I wasn't thinking; it was a mistake.'

'Oh, is that all? In that case, I think I'll go out and have a little mistake myself. Oh, wait. I forgot. I'm already *having* a mistake with Connor, amn't I?'

He doesn't answer.

'You hypocrite. You asshole. Trying to make me feel guilty for something totally innocent when you were having an affair.'

'I genuinely thought…'

'So *this time* you thought? But the *other time* you didn't think?'

'I was worried about us. OK, maybe jealous of Connor, but – the other thing – it just happened. I didn't plan it.'

'Oh well then that's OK.'

'We should see someone.'

I could laugh; I choose to misinterpret. 'You're already seeing someone.'

'I mean a therapist.'

'I thought they were useless.'

'Our marriage is on the line. I'll go to a therapist.'

'Our marriage is *over* the line. It's over, full stop.'

He opens his mouth to speak but I've too much to say.

'I tried to keep it together, Ian. I suggested a therapist, an au pair, a holiday, even going for a bloody night out. But you were too busy – with her.' I will *not* cry. I will *not* give him the satisfaction of that.

'Please, Kim. There has to be a way forward.'

I look at the door. 'There is.'

'I'm not going. This is my home too. I pay the mortgage. I'm the children's father.'

'I don't think the divorce courts will see it that way.'

'Jesus, Kim.'

'Just go. I'll send on your stuff… Malahide, isn't it?'

'What?'

'Malahide. Where James – aka Melanie – lives, yeah?'

'*Melanie?*' He looks confused. 'My secretary? But it's not Melanie.'

I try to hide my shock. I've got this all wrong. 'Who then?'

'Jackie,' he says quietly.

'Your *boss*?'

He looks down and nods.

'Go, Ian. Just get the fuck out, OK?'

This time he does. He actually goes.

And as I hear the front door close, it hits me: I've sent him straight into her arms.

I tell myself I don't care. A woman deserves loyalty; a woman deserves respect.

twenty-five

I wake at 4am, the time I went into labour with both children, the time they used to wake for feeds. Tonight there's no sound. No one breathing beside me. He's with her. I fill my lungs; I have to be strong now, not just for me, but for the kids.

Suddenly, it's not enough that he's physically gone; I want every trace of him gone too. I start to throw open wardrobes and drawers. I fling all his stuff into a heap. There's the shirt he wore at the barbeque. It reminds me of Melanie, whose only fault was her enthusiasm. I mentally apologise to her for all the hate vibes I sent her way.

I tear around the house. Heaps form like molehills. None of the art is his. The furniture is staying put. I remember the golf clubs and fling them onto a pile when really I'd like to wrap them around his neck.

The heap I feel most venomous towards contains *The Investors Chronicle*, *The Economist* and biographies of business tycoons like Warren Buffet, Peter Lynch and Bill Gates. I throw the lot into the fireplace and set it alight. I watch the fire taking hold, curling up the cover of a magazine, discolouring it and finally bursting into coloured flame.

I catch sight of my rings, winking up at me like a rebellion. I wiggle them off. I fling my wedding band into the fire. I hold the engagement ring between my finger and thumb, looking at the stones and remembering what it was like to be so in love that I felt like I could burst. So marriage isn't forever, after all. Diamonds can be, though. I'll get them reset. Turn them into earrings. Or nose rings. Any damn rings I want.

The fire burns out. I head to bed. But can I sleep? Not when I can be imagining him with a brand new mistress, his boss, a successful woman, a stone cold bitch. I think of the hours I've wasted, torturing myself with images of Melanie when all the time the real culprit was dodging my hate vibes. I'll make up for it though. I'll hate her twice as much. But as the sun slowly rises, I come up with a better plan.

At nine, I make a call to my (completely innocent) accomplice. Mum says she'd be *delighted* to mind the children.

I drop them over. Then, music blaring, (Transvision Vamp), I drive into town.

This will be my last time at the offices of AGT Corporate Finance. Good. I hate financial institutions.

Automatic doors part as I enter. Catching my reflection, I look confident and composed. My visit to Wexford has paid off. Hair looks great. As does the red dress. I could pass for an AGT client were it not for the two white sacks slung over each shoulder. I drop them on the ground at reception and announce that I've come to see Ian Kavanagh. Calling him 'my husband' kills me but gives me automatic rights. The receptionist's look doesn't say, 'Oh great, it's Santa Claus,' rather, 'Here's trouble.'

'He's actually in a meeting, Mrs Kavanagh.'

'Waters,' I correct. 'Not Kavanagh.'

She smiles politely. 'Of course. But he can't be interrupted.'

She nods to the boardroom as back up. 'I'll tell him you dropped by. Or you could wait. But it will be a while.'

'Is his boss in there too?' I ask innocently.

'Yes, most of the team.'

Well, *hello Luck,* welcome back. Now, hold on tight. We're going in.

'Excuse me!' the receptionist calls. 'Where are you going, Mrs Kav…?'

All heads pop up as the door crashes back against the wall. I swing one bag into the room, then the other. Stunned silence as I walk to the glass-topped, boardroom table and land the first sack down, wondering how many times her bony ass has fogged it up. The binoculars I bought Ian for his thirtieth birthday shatter the glass like she's shattered my life. I look at her, standing at the head of the table, staring at me like I'm something she scraped off her shoe.

She stares at Ian. 'Get her out of here now!'

Gripping the back of his chair, he quietly says, 'Kim, please.'

Ignoring him, I open the knot on the sack that has wrecked the table. I start to fling his things at her – boxers, ties, tatty, greying vests (bet she hasn't seen these).

Ian starts towards me. 'Kim, please…'

'He's all yours,' I say to her. Then I turn to him. 'It's OK, Ian. I'm leaving. Enjoy the rest of the meeting. Oh and if you're looking for your clubs, they're in the canal.'

I swing the family car out of its space with a screech. I flatten the accelerator, pretending it's his skull. I blast up Alanis Morrisette and shout lyrics that proclaim contempt for and independence of men.

'Were you at a meeting Mum?' asks Chloe, taking in the dress and heels – the Mum she used to know.

'Yes, sweetie and it went really well.' I sound a little hoarse from the singing.

I lift her up and throw her high.

She laughs. 'Again!'

'Me, too,' Sam demands, raising his arms.

I feel a little manic. So I look at Mum to calm me down. I'll have to tell her eventually. I'll have to tell them all. For now, I throw my kids in the air.

The day is fun. I make sure of it. At eight, I crash as two sleepless nights take their toll. But I wake again at four. Nothing I do can get me back to sleep. I relive my performance at AGT Corporate Finance with shame and sadness. What have I turned into?

The door opens. It's Chloe. She climbs in beside me. I cover her up and she goes back to sleep. Her face is soft and pale. Little china doll. One drop and she'll break. How am I going to tell her?

At half-five, I'm awake but groggy when my phone rings. I make a grab for it before it wakes Chloe.

'Kim! I wanted you to be the first to know!' Sarah gushes.

'Sarah, it's five in the morning,' I whisper.

'Ooops, soooorreee, forgot about the time-difference.'

'You're in London. There *is* no time-difference.'

'Actually, I'm in Vegas. You sitting down?'

'Lying down.' And so close to hanging up.

'You're talking to a married woman.'

I sit up.

'Connor and I eloped…'

Connor? Connor and *Sarah*? No *way.*

'You there?' she asks.

'Yeah, yeah, I'm here. Hang on.' I get up, root in the dark for a cardigan and pad out to the landing.

'So, what do you think?' she asks like she can't contain herself.

'I think it's amazing.' As long as it's not one of her jokes… in which case, not funny.

'Imagine! Flying to Vegas like mad young things. I'm still on a high.'

'You went to stay with him for *a week.*'

'I know!'

'Nothing happens that fast.' Except marriage break-ups – they take just twenty-four hours.

'I know, right?'

I open the airing cupboard and search for socks. 'But marriage? I thought you'd given up on the idea?'

'I had. Until Connor. He is *amazing*, Kim.'

'True.' But is he that impulsive? That *mad*?

'Guess who proposed.'

'You?'

She laughs. 'After a weekend of shagadelic sex. And do you know what he said?'

Yes, obviously.

'"Why not?"'

Expressions like, 'lamb to the slaughter', 'look before you leap', and 'Mayday, Mayday', crowd my mind. Everything I admired about Sarah has become a threat. Connor's such a softie. She'll chew him up and spit him out. But maybe I'm wrong, being melodramatic. It could work. Love might conquer all. But I'm not Kim-In-Love, I'm Kim-Will-Never-Love-Again, I'm Kim-What-Is-Love-Anyway? And who-gives-a-fuck? I'm exhausted. It doesn't matter.

'And I've *you* to thank, Kimmy. If I'd stayed in a hotel, we'd never have met. You planned that, didn't you, you little Cupid?'

'No, Sarah, I didn't.'

She gushes on for over an hour. I don't mention that our situations have flipped. Why dent her high? When she finally hangs up, I don't know whether it's the idea that my friends have found love in each other or that Ian is in bed with his boss but I am suddenly the loneliest person in the world. You think you will always matter. And then you don't.

twenty-six

I'm packing a picnic and wondering how a person finds a good lawyer when Connor calls.

'She cast a spell on me,' he jokes. 'I was powerless.' There's a pause. His voice grows serious. 'You don't mind, do you?'

'*Mind*?'

'Me stealing your best friend.'

'I've two best friends. And now they're together. I'm so happy for you both.' I don't add, 'for as long as it lasts,' because that's the cynic in me; it has nothing to do with them.

'Thanks, Kim. Means a lot.'

There's a pause. A gap. A beat. If anyone can help me, it's Connor.

'Con, can I ask you something?' I try to sound light.

'Sure.'

'Do you know any good lawyers in Dublin? I'm looking for one for a friend.'

'What kind of lawyer? Personal injury, conveyancing, family law, employment law?'

'Well, they're splitting up so, family law, I guess.' I try to sound casual.

'What does she want, your friend, a divorce or separation?'

Two words that seem so final. I choke. 'I don't know.'

'Kim, what's wrong?'

I can't speak.

'This friend… It's you, isn't it?'

I bite my hand. Hard.

'Oh God. It *is* you.'

I close my eyes, take a deep breath.

'What happened?'

Suddenly I need to tell someone. 'I kicked him out. He was having an affair.'

'Aw, Kim.'

'I feel like such a fool.'

'I'll kill him.'

'Tempting offer but for now I just need a lawyer, a tough, son-of-a-bitch lawyer.'

'I'm coming home.'

'No. You're on honeymoon. Anyway, Sarah would murder you.' I smile. 'Look, I've done the hardest bit – I've told him to go.'

There's a long pause. Then a sigh. 'All right. Let me get you a number.'

'Thanks, Connor.'

'OK, I'm going to call this guy I know, a legal genius. He's not in family law but he'll know someone good who is.'

'OK, thanks.'

'I'm also sending you the number of a great psychologist.'

'Why would I need a psychologist?' I ask defensively.

'Peter's great, very practical. He'll advise you on what to say to Sam and Chloe and how to cope with their questions. Give him a ring. For advice. Tell him you're a friend of mine.'

I nod. 'Thanks, Con.'

'You sure you're OK?'

'Grand,' I lie. 'And hey, congratulations.'

'You think we're crazy, right?' He's smiling.

'Crazy!' I'm smiling too.

'I'll ...*we'll* be home soon.'

'Well, don't come for me. I'll get this lawyer sorted and I'll be grand. Seriously.'

'I'll call tomorrow. And we'll be home soon, OK?'

'Enjoy your honeymoon.'

Only seven years ago, we were on ours, I think as I hang up. Never did I imagine, when watching Ian by the pool stitching a button onto his trousers so heroically, that it would all be over so quickly.

Then Sarah rings. 'He doesn't deserve you, Kim. Fecker. Seriously. Fecker.'

'I know.' I think of our seven-year marriage and start to cry.

'Aw, Kim.'

'I'm the idiot in your book.'

'No I'm the idiot. Sometimes I think I should staple my mouth shut. I never thought for a moment...'

'That makes two of us,' I say bitterly.

'You did the right thing, telling him to go. Just you wait. He'll come running.'

'No he won't. And I don't want him to.' But part of me does. Part of me wants him to arrive at the door, swoop me up in his arms and tell me it'll be OK, then grab the nearest pair of trousers and stitch a button on – even if it doesn't need it.

'There I was going on about Connor when you guys had just split up. Why didn't you stop me?'

'I was happy for you, Sarah. I wasn't going to ruin it for you.' And then, just so she appreciates what she has, I add, 'You couldn't have picked a nicer guy. You're lucky.'

'I don't deserve him. Or you. Forgive me and my big mouth.'

I smile. 'Part of your charm.'

'I won't let Connor kill him, by the way; I'll get there first.'

I laugh. And feel a little less alone.

'Good girl. You're so independent,' I say to Chloe who needs to learn to dress herself. Fend for herself. Think for herself. Suit herself. Survive. On her own. Take no shit. From anyone. Ever.

We go downstairs together. She skips into the kitchen, so proud of her achievement.

'Where's Dad?' she asks cheerfully.

Oh God. Not now. Not ever, actually. 'At work, honey,' I say lightly. No doubt he is.

'Oh,' she says. 'What's for breakfast?'

'Coco Pops, Ready Brek, Alpen, Cheerios…' Thank God for cereal.

'Melon and then toast with melted butter.'

'Could we be any more specific?'

'What?'

I wink at her. 'Nothing. Sit up at the table.'

Before she's even finished the melon, I've made an appointment with Connor's psychologist.

Next day, I hurry the kids into the car, late for the psychologist's appointment. Across the road, a neighbour gives a cheery wave. Two-to-one Breda O'Neill has already noticed Ian's gone. Seven-to-one she thinks I've murdered him. I return her wavy wave and lift Sam into his car seat.

'Is dis de twain side?' he asks, ensuring that he'll be able to see the train tracks (and a train if possible).

'Yes,' I say.

'But you're getting the mummy side *and* the train side,' whines Chloe.

I ignore them and climb into the front.

'Which would you like best, the mum or the train?' Chloe asks Sam.

'De twain.'

'I'd like the mum,' says Chloe. 'Because I don't like trains.'

Kids – the ultimate confidence booster.

'Chloe, you'll get the mum on the way back,' I say.

I start the car. It lurches forward.

'Chloe! I told you not to touch the controls!'

'The keys weren't in.'

'Regardless of the keys, *never* touch the controls.' I proceed to turn off the fan, headlights, hazard warning lights, blaring radio and window-wipers.

Finally, I check the rear-view mirror. Breda is waving frantically and running up to the car.

What *now*?

I roll down the window. She smiles at me then reaches up over my head.

'Your bag,' she says, retrieving it from the roof.

'God. Thanks, Breda. You're a saviour.' I feel guilty for my earlier thoughts.

'Everything OK? You look a bit distracted.'

OK, that's got rid of the guilt.

'Grand, thanks. Your garden's looking great.' Now get back to it.

'A lot of hard work went into it,' she says proudly.

'Won't keep you. Thanks again.' I smile and start to pull out.

She stands watching us go as though she's outside her own home waving visitors off.

'We will, we will wok you. We will, we will wok you,' Sam shouts from the back. He has learned to sing and wants the world to know. Repetition is all part of the charm. His eclectic mix of favourites includes, 'Runaway Train' (of course), 'Hall of Fame' and, sadly, 'We Will Rock You'.

Chloe joins in.

It's not pretty.

I turn on the radio rather than stifle artistic expression by requesting silence.

Mum looks at me questioningly, no doubt wondering why her child-minding services have been called upon again. I can't tell her. Not now. Not yet. Her marriage was her life.

And I've failed at mine.

I sit in the psychologist's office feeling like I've travelled back in time. The colour scheme is orange and brown. The strip of fluorescent lighting overhead harbours an assortment of dead insects. I can hear a faint buzzing but can't track it down. The walls are dreary, carpets drearier, curtains dreariest. I'm not hopeful.

'And what ages are the children?' the man who looks like Mr Bean asks after I've explained our situation.

'Two-and-a-half and four-and-a-half,' I say, in case the halves make a difference.

'And how much do they know?'

'Nothing. Yet.'

'How much do you think they'll understand?'

'You'd be surprised how clever Chloe is.'

He nods. 'And what do you think she would be comfortable hearing?'

'None of it. But clearly he's gone so I have to say something.'

He nods but fails to volunteer.

'You're the expert,' I prompt.

'Well, in the short-term, the best you can do for the children is provide stability and certainty. For example, they need to know *when* they'll see their dad next. After that, they need to know *how often* they'll see him. It would be good to be able to reassure them about that.'

'But I don't know if he *wants* to see them. Or if *I* want him to.'

'You think he mightn't want to *see* them?' He looks surprised.

'He's shown no interest in them lately.'

He eyeballs me.

'OK, I suppose he'd want to see them,' I admit.

'And what about you? Would you be happy for them never to see their father again?'

'Yes. No. I don't know. I don't want to have to face him. But I know they need to see him.'

He nods. 'How do you think that might work, them seeing him?'

What am I paying this guy for? 'I don't know. I'm getting a lawyer. I presume they'll advise about custody, visitation rights… separation, divorce.' It seems so much. I catch my breath.

'There is the legal option, yes.'

'You don't sound so sure.'

'It's not for everyone. Do you love Ian?'

'Are you joking?'

'Before this.'

'Yes. I did.'

'Do you think that this has changed him as a person?'

'This isn't about *him*. It's about the kids. I just want to know what's best for Sam and Chloe. That's all. That's it. We're going to get through this. We're going to stay strong – and survive this.'

He waits. And waits. Finally: 'And you're sure you want to walk away from your marriage?'

'Sorry. He's the one who walked away.'

'You asked him to leave.'

'Whose side are you on?'

'You came to me because you were concerned about the children. I wouldn't be doing my job if I didn't tell you that what is best for them is a stable environment, ideally with both parents.'

I stare at him.

'I just want to make sure that you've chosen the right path for you. Might you consider listening to what he has to say, coming to see someone like me, together? An affair need not end a marriage. Sometimes it can strengthen it.'

I stand up and grab my bag. 'How much do I owe you?'

'You can talk to my secretary, outside.' He stands. 'I know this is not an easy time. You've been hurt, betrayed…'

'I have and I don't think I'd be giving great example to my children if I was just to lie down and take it! Do you?'

'Reconciliation need not mean submission. It can offer a way to reclaim what you had.' He smiles professionally and extends his hand. 'Please do come back at any time. The door is always open.'

'Thank you.' I'd rather go see the real Mr Bean. At least he'd make me laugh.

twenty-seven

I drive fast. Have I 'stupid' tattooed on my forehead or something? I take Ian back I give him a licence to cheat. I switch on the radio, needing loud music.

What I get – unbelievably – is a discussion on infidelity.

'And why do people have affairs?' the presenter asks the expert.

'Well, Simon, affairs generally begin when a person feels insecure in a relationship, unimportant, unwanted, perhaps unloved. Many describe it as feeling invisible.'

Actually, it's the person who's been cheated on that feels invisible.

'A common scenario is for a father to feel that his partner's main focus of attention is on the children and that there is nothing left for him.'

Yeah, because *the father* is the child.

'Then someone arrives on the scene who makes him feel attractive, desirable, sexy, powerful. Add to that the excitement of having to keep it a secret and you have a heady cocktail.'

Cocktail! It's people's lives he's talking about.

'But it's not all fun and games. There *is* the excitement, absolutely, but there is also the guilt…'

Let's hear how hard it is for cheats. I turn off the radio and honk at the driver in front who is too busy dreaming to pull away from the lights. I've just wasted an entire morning. I have still no idea what to tell the children.

Sam and Chloe are nowhere near ready to leave when I call for them. Mum and I sit on the patio watching them drench themselves, Chloe using a water pistol that's almost bigger than her, Sam the hose. The sun creates rainbows in the mist.

'You OK, love?' Mum asks. 'You look shattered.'

The hair I run my fingers through feels greasy. It reminds me that I'm in need of a good scrubbing. I almost ask her to do it.

'Do you want to go upstairs and lie down? I'll keep an eye on them.'

Suddenly, it just comes out. 'I've left Ian. Well, I told him to leave.'

'What?' she whispers.

'He was having an affair.'

'Oh, Kim. Are you sure?'

I nod.

'How though? Did he admit to it?'

'When his back was to the wall, yeah.'

'Who?' she whispers.

'His boss.'

'His *boss*?' She looks appalled.

'A woman.'

Marginal relief. 'Kim, are you sure about this? It's not like Ian, is it?'

'Ian's human.'

She comes over and gathers me up in her arms. I feel about six.

'How could he, Mum, after all we've shared? The pregnancies, births, first steps, first shoes, first days at Montessori... Whooping cough. Casualty. Dad dying. He was always there.'

'He can be again.'

'No. He's gone. Mentally, physically. I'm not his woman any more. How could he just switch off like that? Wipe out seven years as if they meant nothing?'

'He made a mistake. I'm sure he's sorry.'

'Don't even *think* of making excuses for him.'

'I...'

'Why? Why did he do it? I know I've put on weight. I know I don't dress up. I know the writing hasn't worked out. But I'm still the same person.'

'You are. And you can't blame yourself.'

'Have you looked at me lately? I'm a mess.'

'Of course you're a mess at this very moment. But...'

'I should never have given up work. My confidence is in the toilet.'

She hugs me tighter.

'I didn't flatter him. I didn't tell him how bloody great he was all the time. And I didn't do those pelvic floor exercises.'

'Nobody does, love.'

'I let the children come between us. I always said I'd never let that happen. Wait, you're right. Why am I blaming myself? He's the one who cheated.' I turn to her suddenly. 'Oh my God. What if she has an STD? Syphilis, the clap... Is the clap the same as syphilis?'

'I'm sure they wore protection.'

And then I'm picturing them. 'Comforting thought, Mum.'

She grimaces. 'I knew it sounded wrong as soon as I'd said it.'

'Gonorrhoea.'

'People don't get that any more, love.'

'It's making a comeback!' I panic that he's passed it on, then remember: actually, no problem there.

'Do you still love him?' she asks.

I stare at her. 'How *could* I?'

'Does love go away when someone hurts you?'

'This is more than *hurt*.'

'Have you talked to him, discussed this, given him a chance to explain?'

'Talked to him? I can't even *look* at him.'

'Kim, think about what you have, what you've built together. You're a family, a gorgeous little family. You can't let some hussy just come along and help herself. You have to fight for your family. Not just hand it over.' She delivers this with uncharacteristic passion.

'Why should *I* do all the fighting? Anyway, I've none left. I'm tired of fighting.'

She sighs deeply and sits back at the table.

We look at the children who are now standing perfectly still, heads bent as they refill the water pistol using the hose.

'I didn't want this for you,' Mum says.

'I didn't either,' I joke. Then it hits me. 'Why would you have even *thought* about this for me? Were there *signs*? Was there something *wrong* with us?'

She shakes her head. 'No. Doesn't stop it happening.'

'Since when did you become a pessimist?'

Chloe screeches.

'Sam, your sister is not a fire. Take it easy,' I say.

'It's OK, Mum,' she calls. 'I like it.'

I smile.

'So he's actually gone?' Mum asks.

'Yeah.'

'Where?'

I shrug.

'Kim.'

'Kim what? Fuck him. You think I care where he's gone?'

'*Do* you?'

'I need a coffee.' I stand up and go inside.

I hold onto the worktop and take deep breaths. I don't care. I don't care. I don't care where he's gone.

But I do care – if he's with her.

Shit.

I hide out in the kitchen until the coffee is ready. I inhale its smell as if it will provide inner strength. Then I brace myself and go back outside.

She is drying the kids off and wrapping them in towels.

'My little angels,' she is saying. 'Here, let's put on your hoodies and you can go play in the sand.'

Then they're off again. The energy. It's exhausting.

Mum comes back to the patio.

For a while we sit in silence.

Then she looks at me. 'When you told him to leave, what did he say?'

'Does it matter?'

'Did he say he was sorry?'

'Don't they all?'

'No, Kim, they don't.'

'What would *you* know? With your perfect marriage.'

She raises an eyebrow. 'No marriage is perfect. Not one.'

I tighten my fingers around my mug wishing it were his neck.

'Did he say he'd stop seeing her?'

'Mum, I don't want to do this.'

'But *I* do. It's important. So. Did he?'

'Yeah but so what?'

'What do you want, Kim?'

'I don't want him back, that's for sure.'

'Do you love him?'

'This again? He cheated. End of story.'

'People cheat. For lots of reasons. Doesn't mean it has to be over.'

'I take him back, I may as well lie on the ground and say, "walk all over me".'

'It's called forgiveness.'

'Jesus, Mum.'

'What do you want, Kim? You have to ask yourself that – I mean really ask yourself – before it's too late. Before he's gone for good. What, do, you, want?'

'I can't *have* what I want. I can't go back to the way it was. So what I want doesn't matter, does it? It certainly doesn't matter to him. He's made *that* clear.'

'You want your life back. OK.'

My laugh is bitter. 'Yeah. Just like that.'

She sighs. 'Well, I'd like mine back too but death is non-negotiable. I'll never see your father again. I wake to rediscover that, every day.'

'I'm sorry. I didn't mean to…'

'You and Ian have a chance. I'm not going to say it'll be easy. But you have your lives ahead of you. You have the kids – who need their parents, Kim. And you have your love for each other.'

'*Do* we?'

'He made a mistake.'

'A mistake! Dad would *never* have "made a mistake".'

She looks away. Too quickly.

'What?'

'Nothing.'

'What is it?' Jesus. 'Mum?'

She swipes at the tear. Then another.

'Mum?'

'You've always been so stubborn. To you, there's only ever one way. Ian said he was sorry; he said it was over. He's a good man. You love each other. Take him back, for God's sake, before it's too late and he decides he doesn't want to come back.'

'I can't.'

'You can. I did. You can.'

'What? What did you say?' I'm asking but suddenly I don't want to know.

She looks down. Her shoulders rise as she takes a deep breath. Then she looks at me. 'I didn't want to tell you because I know how you worshipped him.' She looks at me.

'No. No way. Not Dad. He'd never…'

'And yet he did.'

Silence now as questions flood my mind. When did this happen? Who with? For how long? How did Mum find out? What did she do? How didn't I notice? Did James? Poor Mum.

'Life's not as simple as you think,' she says. 'There's more to a man than his mistakes. Your father was a good person and a great dad. Yes, he had an affair, but should that be the only thing to consider? Just that one thing?'

'I think it's relevant.' Very fucking relevant.

'Would you have forgiven me if I'd just demanded he leave?'

'Yes, Mum, I would.'

'Really? Think about that. If I had, you'd never have known him.'

I stare at her. 'Wait, that means he had the affair when I was very young?'

'Yes and think what you'd have missed if I'd made it the most important thing about him?'

'How could you forgive him?'

'I loved him,' she says like it's the simplest thing in the world. 'I loved him and I didn't want to lose him. I wanted us to stay a family. It was the most important thing to me. It still is. I'm glad I did what I did. I've never regretted it.'

'Tell me about it.'

She looks at me for a long time. 'On one condition. You have to remember the good in him, how much you loved him, how much he loved you. Because if you start hating him, everything I've done will have been a waste.'

'I'll try.'

'Promise me, Kim,' she demands.

'OK, I promise.' To try.

'I don't want you telling James.'

'James is part of the family. You can't keep it from him.'

'Promise me, Kim. Not a word to James. Or I'll take this with me to my grave.'

'Don't say grave.'

'Promise me or I'll say no more.'

'OK. I promise.'

'Your father was a good man who was unlucky enough to fall in love with two women.'

'Don't tell me you swallowed that one.'

'Do you want to hear or not?'

'OK. Sorry,' I grumble.

'He fell in love with another woman, a friend of ours.'

'Who?'

'Kim, will you let me tell this my own way, please?'

'Sorry.'

'When you were born, there were problems; you know that. You and I had to stay in hospital for two months.'

I nod. She's told me.

'It was touch and go for both of us for a while. Dad was in a desperate state. On top of that he had to mind James. I asked a friend to help him out. She was always so capable…'

One word for it.

'But something happened that I never expected. Their friendship turned to love. When we were discharged and I came home with my little girl, you,' she smiles, reaches out and holds my hand, 'they told me immediately.' She lets me go, sits back and looks into the distance.

If I hadn't been born, this would never have happened.

'So I do know what you're feeling, Kimmy. Except you're lucky: Ian wants to stay with you. Your father wanted to continue seeing this woman. He said that he loved her and wanted to be with her and if he couldn't, he'd leave. I was hysterical. Didn't know what to do. I told him to give me a week to think. I didn't want to lose him. I loved him. And I wanted my family to stay together. So I came up with an idea. A deal. I told him he could go on seeing her but with conditions.'

'*What* conditions?' I don't believe this. This is not my mum.

'Firstly, he'd continue to live at home. Secondly, he'd only see her at regular, allotted times; there would be no sneaking around, no surprise disappearances. He would be there for all important family occasions and always if you were sick.'

'What regular allotted times? I don't remember him being away at all.'

'Every Friday night he'd stay with her and come back early Saturday morning. And every six weeks he'd stay for a weekend.'

'Oh my God. So those trips to London weren't to London?' I feel so stupid.

'No.'

'He was doing this all my life?'

She nods.

'I hate him.'

She smiles. 'No. You don't.'

'He treated you like shit.'

'Those were *my* terms. I got what I wanted. It wasn't the traditional way to live but it was my way. Yes, in an ideal world, he'd have been just mine but that wasn't an option and I had him most of the time. *We* had him most of the time.'

'My childhood was a lie,' I whisper.

'Stop.' She slaps her hand down on the table. 'Stop seeing the world only from your point of view. Stop making rules for everyone else. Stop expecting too much from people. We're all human. We're all just doing our best.'

This person is not my mum.

'You were a happy child who grew up in a loving environment with people who loved you and each other. It wasn't orthodox. But it was real. Very real. Remember the good in your father. There was plenty.'

Yeah, like his ability to have his cake and eat it. 'Who was she?' I must know her, if she was their friend. I must know her.

'I'd rather not say. I don't see how it would help.'

'Tell me. No more secrets. Just tell me.'

'You have to promise not to do anything. Not to let on to her that you know. And not ever to tell another living soul. This woman is in the public eye.'

Who the hell is it? 'I promise.'

She takes a deep breath. 'It was Deirdre French.'

'Deirdre French? The novelist?'

She nods.

'But you're still friends.'

'Acquaintances who are, on the surface, friendly, yes.'

'I asked her for help! You sent me to her! You think I'd have gone if I'd known? My God, Mum. I have my pride.'

'That is *exactly* your problem.'

I stare at her. Who is this person?

'She owed us,' she says simply.

'I'm sorry but this is so messed up. Seriously. The woman has everything – success, fame, fortune – and she had to have my father too?'

'You're wrong. She doesn't have everything. Don't you see? She loses. She has nothing. No family, no husband, no children. Another part of the deal – they agreed never to have children – your dad was only ever to be a father to you and James. Deirdre French has nothing. She's a lonely woman. If you want to feel sorry for someone – feel sorry for her.'

'Well, I don't. Look what she took from you.'

'Nothing, that's the point. I didn't throw away my husband, lose the father of my children, like you're doing. I kept it all. I won.'

'Why did he stay with us? Why didn't he just go off with her if he loved her so bloody much?'

'Because he loved us too. He loved you and James. And he loved me. We just learned to share. You don't have to, Kim; you can have Ian to yourself. Don't you see? You're one of the lucky ones.'

'This is like something out of a Deirdre French novel.'

She looks at me. 'It *is* a Deirdre French novel. *The Deal.*'

'You're fucking kidding me?'

She shakes her head.

'Oh my God. Living off us, rubbing our nose in it…'

'Read it, Kim. It explains a lot. It's her confession.'

'Taking a psychological dump on us and making a profit as well. I have to hand it to her.'

'When did you become so cynical?'

'Not soon enough, Mum. Not soon enough.'

'I shouldn't have told you.'

'You absolutely bloody should.'

'So you'll take him back?'

'I don't see how the two are connected. Apart from me being surrounded by cheating men.'

'I only told you so you'd see how lucky you are.'

Lucky is not how I feel. I stand up before I fall down. 'I've a lot to think about, OK?'

'You won't tell James, will you, love?'

'No, Mum. I won't tell James.'

She lets out a long breath. Then she stands too. 'Are you all right?'

'Not particularly, no.'

'I'm sorry for snapping at you.'

'OK. Listen, I gotta go.'

She reaches out and holds my hand. And it strikes me: I've known this woman thirty-four years without knowing her at all.

twenty-eight

I set Sam and Chloe up on the couch with pillows and a quilt. I put on *The Little Mermaid*.

'I'm just going upstairs for a minute,' I say.

But they don't hear me.

I climb into bed feeling like I've been stepped on. I go over events from my past and see them as they really were. Birthday parties, holy communions, confirmations.... He was there because he had to be. I get up and root out old family albums. I check the background of every shot for any trace of Deirdre French. What would she have looked like, then? Glamorous, no doubt. Thinner maybe. Elegant. But I don't find her ghost. That was probably part of The Deal too. Not to come near us. I wonder what *he* thought when *The Deal* was published? Did they argue about it? Or did he forgive her everything? I gaze at a photo of him, standing behind James and me, a hand on each of our shoulders, as if to say, 'These are my children of whom I am proud.' I have always loved this picture. Was it taken on a Friday – before he left us for her?

He died on a Friday. Did she get to say goodbye? Did she creep into the hospital under cover of darkness? Did she feel the pain I did? Hope so. Hope she still feels it. Hope it keeps her awake at night. When I spoke to her that time, she asked how my mum was. Wow. The nerve of that.

My phone vibrates, reminding me that I put it on silent before going in to see the psychologist. There are six messages. The first three are from Ian and all say the same thing: he's sorry; it's over; and we have to talk. The next message is from Connor; he's coming to Dublin. A text from Mum is irrelevant because we've seen each other since. The last message is from Ian asking me to call him.

Easier to make dinner. Keep busy.

The fridge contains an empty milk carton, blue cheese (that's meant to be orange), expired yoghurts, a sad lettuce and a bottle of wine. With a sigh, I go to get my bag. Then I stop. What if he's cancelled the credit card? He wouldn't. He wants to talk. Still, I can't risk loading up a supermarket trolley, children in tow, only to be turned away at the checkout.

I could call him. But that is the last thing I want to do.

Finally, I hit on a solution. Takeaway! I order over the phone, remain invisible and discover that, hallelujah, the credit card still works.

My relief doesn't last long. He could cancel it at any time.

For now, the pizzas arrive.

Afterwards, the children make history by asking to go to bed. They're asleep almost immediately.

I'm sampling one of the contents of the fridge (not the lettuce) when the doorbell goes. I put down my glass, thinking: Ian.

It rings again.

Shit. He'll wake the children.

At the door, I inhale deeply. Then I open it.

The relief.

'Connor!'

Suspended in the warm evening air are all things yet to be said. So much has changed, our positions reversed, overnight, almost. He lowers his bags and hugs me. I try – so hard – not to cry. At last, I pull back.

'Where's Sarah?'

He smiles. 'Her publishers went ballistic when they discovered she'd taken off in the middle of her publicity tour. They said she was in breach of contract and better get back to London ASAP. So that's where she's headed. She's so sorry she can't be here but she'll ring in the morning.'

'You needn't have come.'

'I wanted to. We have a pact, remember?'

I think of the other pact, The Deal. Then try to forget about it again.

We negotiate scattered toys, children's clothes, shoes and unfinished Liga to reach the kitchen.

'Sorry. The place is a mess.'

'I think you're entitled to a mess.'

'You look so happy.'

'You know me, always happy.'

He's joking but it's actually true. Probably the most positive person I know.

I see him glance at the wine on the table.

'Damn. I've nothing to offer you, no Coke, no juice. I need to go shopping.'

'Do you've tea?'

'Of course.'

'You have *no idea* how much a man can miss a proper cup of tea.'

I go to make it but he raises a hand. 'Sit. I've been on planes for sixteen hours. I can't feel my limbs.'

I sit at the table and top up my glass.

'So did you speak to Peter?' he asks of the 'psychologist'.

'Yeah. He wanted me to get back with Ian. I mean, for Christ's sake.'

He looks surprised. 'What did he say about telling Sam and Chloe? Did he have any advice on that?'

I sigh. 'He said to give them security by telling them when they'll see their father.'

'Sounds reasonable.'

'Only I haven't spoken to Ian since the punch-up at his office on Tuesday.'

'Punch-up?'

I close my eyes. 'OK don't judge me.' I fill him in.

He listens incredulously, then laughs. 'Go you.'

'No. I should have held onto my dignity. It's all I've bloody left.'

'You have Sam and Chloe.'

'Who need their father. What if I've ruined it for them?' I think of Mum and how big she was, really. How powerful. In her own quiet way.

'You're not the one at fault, here. Did you get on to the lawyer?'

'Not yet.'

'Want me to call him?'

'No. I'll do it,' I say, instead of, 'please go.' It's too much. It's all too much.

'Let's go inside,' he suggests.

I don't forget the wine.

In the sitting room, I turn around. But he's not there.

He appears then with duty-free bags. 'Thought you might need some cheering up.'

He sits on the couch and starts to produce a range of pampering products from Molton Brown, which, one by one, he places on the table. The last one out is a massive candle. 'Got a lighter?'

Doesn't he see that he's moving deckchairs on a sinking ship?

'I don't know. Try the third drawer in the kitchen. If we, I, have one, it'll be there.'

He comes back holding one to the sky.

I smile but I'm just so tired.

'So. What are we celebrating?' he asks.

'The newly-weds.' I raise my glass. 'To Connor and Sarah. A long and happy life together.'

He smiles. 'To Connor and Sarah. What *were* they thinking?'

And suddenly I feel so much love and hope for them. I take a sip of wine, then circle my shoulders. Everything's so stiff.

'You know what you need? A Connor special.'

'What's that?'

'A head massage.'

I laugh.

'I'm serious. Bet you've a headache.'

My head has been pounding since Discovery Number One. I'm amazed I still have a head since Number Two. 'A bit.'

'Right, sit back and I'll come at you from behind.'

I laugh. 'Sorry.'

'Such a child.'

We take up our positions.

'Now, just let your mind go blank. Empty it completely. Actually, hang on. Where did I leave my phone?'

Soon, lovely soothing pan-pipey music floats on the air. And I know I'm in good hands.

He applies gentle but firm pressure to my scalp with his fingertips. He works in circular movements until he has covered my whole head. I feel the tension ease. He stops.

I open my eyes. 'Is that *it*?'

'No. That's not *it*. I need to get at you from the front.'

I laugh. 'Connor. Seriously. Change your vocab.'

'Can't help your filthy mind.' He takes the body oil from the table, tips it into his hands and rubs them together. I close my eyes and inhale deeply. I feel like I am in a spa. This *is* good.

I feel the cushion lower as he kneels beside me. He starts to work on my forehead. Oh my God. It's so good. His thumbs circle my temples, easing the tension there. I could fall asleep. He moves to my cheeks and finally the area around my mouth, which he circles with a finger. It feels sensual. I find myself blushing. I force my eyes to stay closed.

Connor is my friend, my very platonic friend, my very married platonic friend.

I open my eyes and utter an embarrassed, 'That's great, Connor,' to wrap it up.

But I catch him looking down at me with such tenderness that even I, in my numbed state, see it. He shuts it off immediately. But knows he's been caught. Neither of us speaks. Seconds feel like days.

Then he stuns me with, 'I love you, Kim. Always have. Since the moment we met.'

I stare at him, trying to take it in.

'But you were always with someone else and so was I. One of us was always with someone. And still, somehow, I believed we'd end up together. Then you met Ian and I knew, everyone knew, that was it. I told myself it wouldn't last but didn't really believe it. I came to your wedding, hugged you, congratulated you and smiled a lot. I got on with my life, met other women, lots of other women, even got married.' He smiles sadly. 'It was all working out. Until you opened your eyes.'

I don't know what to say.

'If I'd thought for one second that you'd ever be free again, I'd never have married. That's the truth.'

'But you are married, Connor. And so am I.' Officially.

He sighs so deeply. 'I know.'

Silence.

'Can I kiss you, Kim? Just once.'

'No,' I say but it's a yes and we both know it. One kiss won't change anything.

But it does. It leads to another. And another. And another. Until they melt into one, long passionate embrace. I let go, don't care any more, don't care about anything. This man loves me. That's all that matters.

His hand supports the back of my neck, his fingers stretching out into my hair as he plants kiss after kiss on my face then throat until he reaches that spot where a vampire sinks its teeth in. Do it, I think. Bite me dead. His excitement arouses me. He wants me.

And I want him. I want it. Or maybe I just want someone to want me. Oh, I don't care.

I lie back.

His hands are everywhere. His mouth. And the pressure of his body on mine. Our legs entangle. Our hips press together. I whisper, 'please.' One by one, and slowly, he undoes the buttons on my shirt, planting a kiss on my skin where each one used to be, like an explorer leaving a flag on each spot he's conquered. I wriggle out of my shirt and tear at his. How have I never noticed his body? He is Michelangelo's David. Perfection. There is something powerful about the way he unbuckles his belt. Then pop, pop, pop go the buttons on his jeans and there he is in all his glory.

I've never had sex sitting up. There's a lot to be said for it. Like 'Oh my God,' and 'Oh Jesus,' and 'Oh Connor,' and a groaned, 'Kiiiim', as he comes. He turns me over and starts to drive me wild. What is he *doing*? Jesus, it's bottom bites, thousands of tiny bottom bites. And there I was sorry I had an ass at all. This changes everything. High Ho Silver! What is happening to me? What kind of weirdo am I becoming? But I get what Sarah sees in him after so many men – he is instinctive, knowing what I like even though I don't. Sarah. Don't think of Sarah. Oh God, Sarah. What are we doing?

The next, 'What are we doing?' is said aloud and it breaks the spell. There is a fumbling with clothes and more with words.

'I'm sorry,' he utters. 'I didn't mean....'

'Sarah!' I say. 'God. What have we done?' I'm surrounded by cheats. I'm a cheat; Connor's a cheat; Ian's a certified cheat. My father cheated for twenty-nine years. But I'm the worst because I cheated *knowing* what it does to the people you love. I've deceived Sarah, my family, myself. Not Ian. I haven't cheated on Ian because how can you cheat on a cheat?

Just one week. That's all it took for my life to unravel.

twenty-nine

I wake at six. And go downstairs. Connor, supposed to be asleep on the couch, is in the kitchen nursing a mug of coffee and looking so miserable it's almost funny.

'We need help,' he says.

'Speak for yourself.'

'I'm serious. We need to understand what happened here.'

'We fucked up. That's what happened.' Holding my head, I find juice and a painkiller.

'What if it happens again?'

'It won't.'

'How do you know?'

'Connor, I know. For starters, I was drunk.'

'I wasn't. What's my excuse?'

'I don't know. What *is* your excuse?' I turn on him. It's the easiest thing to do.

'I have none. That's why we should see someone.'

'Then *you* see someone.'

'Look, Kim. I've thought about this all night and keep coming back to the same thing. We won't be able to stay friends unless we sort this out. And we won't sort it out on our own. Look at us now, for Christ's sake. You can't even look at me. If I walk out of here now and pretend this never happened, I won't be able to look you in the eye again which means I won't be able to see you again without Sarah knowing. And that's not on. It's not on for Sarah.'

I look at him.

'Please, Kim. For Sarah.'

This is so weird. 'When you say help, you better not mean Peter. I'm not going back to him. On principle.'

'I *was* thinking of Peter. He was great with my… problem.'

'Not mine.'

'Because he told you something you didn't want to hear.'

'You're right. I didn't want to hear that I should forgive and forget so I can be walked on again.' I go to the sink and clatter around not knowing exactly what I'm doing.

He comes over. Then he's tearing off a sheet of kitchen paper and handing it to me.

'Peace offering.'

I take it from him and blow my nose. I look out at my neglected garden.

'We could go together,' he says. 'For moral support.'

'That would be a first – therapy for a couple married to two separate people.'

'Will *you* be able to look Sarah in the eye? Because *I* won't.'

I sigh deeply.

'He never judges, just tries to understand and help you sort it out for yourself.'

'That's not how it felt to me.'

'Will you give it a try? Just once. Please. For Sarah. For all of us. If it doesn't work out, it doesn't work out. And we'll know we did our best. OK?'

I look down at the white line on my wedding finger. Then I look up at him. I want one of our marriages to work.

'All right.'

'Aw, great.' He sounds so relieved. 'Thanks, Kim. I'll ring Peter.'

'Warn him not to bring up Ian.'

'Is, is, is today summa school, Mum?' asks Sam, who has just shuffled in, rubbing his eyes. The sight of him in all his innocence makes me want to lift him up and say over and over, 'Mummy is sorry. Mummy didn't mean it.' Instead it's, 'Yes, pet.'

'Aw.'

'Last day, sweetie. Tomorrow's Saturday and then you'll have a whole week off before you go back to Montessori.' I can't believe that Chloe is starting school – and that her father will miss it. He probably wouldn't have made it anyway, even if we were still a family.

'Don't want Chlo to go to big school. Want Chlo to stay with Sam.' He looks at Connor and then me.

'Whay's my dad?'

'Guess,' I say.

'Wuk.'

A wink is not technically a lie.

'My dad's always at wuk.' His head flops down, as do the corners of his mouth. He kicks the air.

'Say hi to Connor.'

'Hi.' Another kick.

'Do you want a drink of apple juice?' I ask to distract him.

'Yeah.'

'Yes, please.'

'Yes, please.'

'What do you want for breakfast?'

'Poo poo.'

I smile in relief, then offer his favourite cereals. Ian wouldn't know his favourites if they came up and bit him. I'd like something to bite *him*, something big. Like a killer whale. Or a lot of small somethings (ideally piranhas).

'Toast,' says Sam.

I pop bread in the toaster. 'Is Chloe awake?'

He doesn't reply. He has found Percy The Tank Engine.

I head upstairs, preparing for objection. My daughter does not like to be woken.

But she is already up and getting dressed. 'Is Dad downstairs?' she asks with a hope that pierces my heart.

'No, sweetheart, he's at work.' He probably is by now.

'But I heard him!'

'No, sweetheart – that's Connor.' Normally that'd be enough to send her running downstairs. Not today.

'Mum, Dad works too hard.'

'I know, sweetie. But you'll see him soon.' *Why* did I say that?

'Today?'

'We'll see. Come on, let's get brekkie.' We go downstairs holding hands.

And I feel so guilty that I haven't been able to hold our little family together.

A cancellation. Connor and I are seen first thing. Our behaviour is analysed, explanations given. I can't argue with mine: I was feeling lonely, discarded; I needed someone to show me love. Connor needed 'closure' on his infatuation with me before he could move on with Sarah. We are lucky – apparently – that we came to him at this stage (he loves himself) because everything can still work out for the newly-weds. Connor needs to get back to London and make it work. And, wait for it, we should *not* confess.

'But we'd be living a lie!' Connor says.

My exact thought sounds so melodramatic when expressed.

'Would you rather wound those you love? What would telling them achieve?'

I don't know why he's looking at me. I don't love Ian. And I'm not telling him a thing. He deserves nothing from me, least of all to know what I do with my time.

'So you recommend deceit?' Connor asks, cynically.

'What you have done is deceitful. But it's done and you can't erase it. Telling them about it will only hurt. You are the only two who know what happened. They will never find out. Keeping it to yourselves will be harder on you than on them. Kim!'

I jump.

'Perhaps now you can understand how easy it is for affairs to happen?'

'Last night was an accident and we're here to make it right. What Ian did was ongoing and underhand. He lied to me, repeatedly. He spent our money on her while telling me to cut back. He made me feel small. I don't know how you can compare them.'

'If you had not come here today, you might have gone on to have an affair.'

I shake my head.

'Mistakes are what make us human. I'm sure Ian is crippled with guilt; he has lost his family.'

'He deserves every bit of goddamn guilt he feels.'

'But maybe now you can understand why he had the affair?'

'No. Actually.' I shift in my chair and tap my fingers. Can we be finished?

'Do you think the reasons for his affair may have been any different from yours?'

'Firstly, I didn't have an affair. Secondly, of course they're different. Completely different.'

'Don't you think he might have been feeling like you felt? Lonely, isolated, unloved, unneeded?'

'Ian *was* loved. We all loved him. He just didn't want us. We weren't enough. If he was lonely it was his own doing – he never came home.'

'Maybe it was you he was lonely for.'

'I was *there*.'

'But were you there for him?'

'*Yes.*'

'Not busy with the children?'

'I was busy. But I loved him. He knew that.'

'Maybe he didn't. Maybe he felt you loved the children more.

It happens all the time. Maybe he needed to be reminded of your love.'

Why are we seeing a male psychologist? '*Look*, Ian got bored. Wanted something new. Like your typical selfish bastard.'

'How are the children taking the news?'

When I hesitate, Connor lets the truth be known.

'She hasn't told them.'

'I understand that this is hard but, for the sake of the children, can I suggest that you take Ian's next call? You need to discuss the future, especially in terms of him seeing the children, and financial matters. Both you and the children need certainty in your lives. I wouldn't let it go on any longer.'

I sigh deeply. Then nod. Because I can kick and scream all I want. The man is right.

We finish up and pay the secretary. Then Connor suggests coffee.

.

thirty

In a nearby café, Connor looks at me.

'That was great,' he says like he's just taken a dump.

'*Was* it?'

'Come on, Kim. It was really helpful. He makes so much sense.'

'So your conscience is clear?' Men.

'No. It's not clear. But Peter's right. We all make mistakes. It's life. And we have to learn to live with it.' He produces a simple smile as if everything has suddenly become that way. 'How about you?'

'I don't want to talk about it.'

'What he said about Ian – and the kids – it makes sense.'

'You see a shrink and suddenly you become one.' I look out at the people passing and want to be them, any of them. I'm not fussy.

'What are you going to do?' he asks.

I turn to him. 'Arrange for them to see him, I suppose.'

'Good.'

'Just wish I could do it without having to face him myself.'

'Maybe you can.'

'No. Any other option would seem unnatural to Sam and Chloe. And I want everything to feel as normal as possible.'

'When are you going to call him?'

'I'm not. He can call me.'

'Oh.' He looks like he's worried that marriage is more complicated than he thought.

'Anyway. No use sitting here all day talking about it. You've a flight to catch.'

He nods. Then books it on his phone.

Outside the café, he strides to the nearest taxi rank. He doesn't look back.

I'm walking to the car when my phone rings. I look at Ian's cheating face on the screen. I close my eyes, take a deep breath and force myself to answer.

'Hello, Ian.'

'Oh, Kim. Hi. Thank God. I thought you'd never talk to me.'

'Don't tempt me.'

'How are you?'

'Fine.'

'The children?'

'They're fine – because I haven't told them.'

'Please don't.'

'Ian, they're not stupid. They *do* notice you're missing.'

'We could tell them together.'

Like it's good news. I bite down on a finger.

'Kim, I need to see them.'

'*You* need?'

'I'm sorry but they need to see me too. I'm their father.'

'Interesting how you remember that now.'

'Can I come over this afternoon?'

'No.' I pause. 'You can come at seven. See them for an hour.

Then, when they're in bed, we can talk about custody and finances.' I hope I sound cold, factual and detached because I feel the opposite. These are our children. We were a family.

'Seven's fine,' he chokes. I'm about to hang up when he jumps in with, 'Kim, what will we say to them? How will we tell them? We should sing from the same hymn sheet...'

Hymn sheet, Jesus. 'You think of something, Ian. You'll be doing the talking.'

'I'd like to tell them I'll be home soon.'

'You want to lie to them? I don't think so, Ian.'

'I was hoping...'

'Well don't. I'll see you at seven.' I hang up. My hand is shaking and when I reach the car, I steady myself with it.

'Is it seven yet?' Chloe asks for the hundredth time.

I nod. 'It's seven.'

She and Sam race to the front room. Sam climbs up on the couch and stands peering over its back, giving him a view of the driveway. Chloe takes up position at the window. Their enthusiasm is heartbreaking.

I know he's arrived when Sam starts jumping up and down. And Chloe runs to me.

'It's Dad! It's Dad! Open the door, Mum.'

'It's OK, sweetie. He has a key.' Then I think: If he uses it, I *will* kill him.

The doorbell rings.

'Mum! Mum! It's Dad.' They run out into the hall.

I must have raced to the door too when I was young. For my cheating father.

I get up slowly, breathing deeply and repeating the mantra, I can do this. Last time I saw Ian – at the office – I was all drama and emotion. Today, I will be dignified.

Chloe runs in, grabs my hand and tugs me forward. '*Mum!*'

'I'm coming.'

In the hall, Sam is jumping to reach the catch on the front door. He is calling his father.

What are we doing to them?

Before I have the door fully open, they dash out and grab his legs. They cling to him, each trying to outdo the other with their 'Dads' and stories.

I stand, holding the door. I'm aiming for dignified but it's hard.

He looks up from where he has hunched down to hug our babies. Days ago, this man was my husband. A week ago, everything was normal. Or at least I thought it was.

He looks shaken, like he did when he lost his father to leukaemia. His eyes are so sad that I have a moment of weakness. Luckily it passes and I return his look with one of ice.

He lifts them up, one in each arm. I want to ruin the moment for him but can't because I would ruin it for them too. And as he kisses each of them on the forehead I look on like I'm watching a scene from a movie that isn't my life.

He looks at me as if to say: Can I come in?

I stand back. He lets the kids down and they torpedo in, Chloe grabbing him by the hand to make sure he comes.

'I'll be in the kitchen if you need me,' I say.

He gets the message but the children don't.

'Mu..um. We want you too.' It's Sam.

Chloe says nothing but looks from Ian to me then back to Ian again.

They know. Somehow, they know.

So I give them what they want, my presence in the room. But I pick the chair furthest from the happy family scene.

'Look Dad, Thomas is bwoken,' says Sam, referring to his tank engine.

It's as if nothing has happened, as if I've imagined it all. And I wish... No I don't.

'Hmm. Let's see. Maybe he needs new batteries.' Ian looks at me as if to say, 'have we got any?'

The old me would have jumped into action. The new me keeps her eyes blank. Let him work it out.

He's stuck. Can't go tracking down batteries without trespassing.

But Sam is looking at his dad, The Fixer, with a mixture of admiration and impatience.

Damn. 'They're in the kitchen in the third drawer,' I say looking away. Then I remember Connor. I directed him to the same drawer only last night.

Ian disappears, the children in his wake.

My phone starts to ring. I check the screen.

Oh God. It's Sarah.

I am halfway up the stairs before I answer.

'Hey!' she says cheerfully.

And I breathe again.

'How are you?' she asks.

Guilty as hell. 'Fine. Thanks. You?'

'*So* glad to have Connor back. We were apart one day, *one day,* and I missed him so much. He's *so* special, Kim. How could you have kept him from me all this time?'

'Sarah, this isn't a great time.'

'Oh sorry. I was just calling to see how you are. Everything OK? You poor thing.'

Downstairs, Ian, playing with the children, laughs out loud.

I sigh.

'What is it?'

'Nothing. Ian's here.'

'You didn't take him *back*, did you?'

'No. He's here to see the children. And to sort out custody.'

'Good. Don't let him push you around.'

'Yeah, I've got to go, here.'

'Hang on a sec. Connor wants a word.'

'Tell him I'll call him back, OK?'

'Oh. OK.'

thirty-one

Ian puts the children to bed. When he comes back down, he seems to have forgotten how things are, walking into the room wearing a big smile.

'He's really obsessed with the old trains, isn't he?'

I raise a cool eyebrow.

He loses the smile. 'Kim, I can't tell you how sorry...'

'We're all sorry.'

He sits near me. 'How are you?'

Hurt, tired, sad, lonely. But I just look at him coldly. 'Did you tell them?'

He shakes his head. 'I couldn't do it to them. They seemed so happy.'

'Well, you're going to have to!'

'We can't wake them up now!'

'They're not asleep.'

'I'll tell them next time. I promise.'

'Next time?'

He looks panicked.

'It's all right.' I sigh. 'I was joking.'

He looks weary.

'Let's talk custody,' I say, wanting him gone.

He nods.

'Well?' I say.

'Well, what?'

'I don't know. I haven't done this before.'

'Neither have I.' He attempts a smile.

'We need lawyers.'

'Maybe we can work it out without lawyers.'

'What do you suggest?'

'Well, couldn't we work something out that suits us both?'

'Like?'

'I don't know. We could start by seeing if you agree with how often I'd like to see them?'

'And how often *would* you like to see them?'

'Um.' He rubs his forehead. He looks at a stain in the carpet then back at me. 'I'd like to see them every week, of course. I'd *love* to see them a little every day but that probably wouldn't suit you so what about at least once during the week and maybe take them every second weekend? And the weekends I'm not taking them, maybe I could see them for an afternoon or two? Would that be OK with you?' He looks hopeful.

And I can't believe we're doing this. Dividing out our children. I feel like giving in, telling him he can see them whenever he wants. But this is the man who wants it all.

'I can't let you take them at the weekends when I don't know where you'll be.'

'The Lansdowne Hotel.'

'You're staying in a hotel?'

'It's not too expensive and it's near work.'

Where she is. 'I don't want them to meet her.' I feel like my mother. Making The Deal.

'I'm not seeing her, Kim.'

'I don't care what you do with your life as long as you don't do it in front of our children.' And I wish that this were true. It will be, though, in time.

'It's over with her.'

I shrug like I don't care. 'Ian, I'm not going to come between you and the children. You can see them as often as you want – as long as it's just you.'

'Thank you,' he says hoarsely and he starts to well up.

'Don't thank me. I'm doing it for them.'

'Thanks, anyway. You didn't have to be fair. You could have kept them from me. To punish me. I know that. So thank you.'

'I don't want them hurt. I don't even want to tell them.'

'Maybe we don't have to. Maybe we could pretend. They're so small. So vulnerable.'

'I wish you'd thought of that. I wish you'd thought of them. Of me.' I get up and hurry from the room.

In the bathroom, I wash my face, blow my nose and avoid the mirror. He knows not to come after me. But suddenly I want him to. I want him to take me in his arms and promise me that we'll go back to the start and he'll be around all the time and we'll do things together. But if he said that, I wouldn't believe him. I take a deep breath and go back out.

He's fiddling with little windmills Sam and Chloe made at summer camp.

He looks up. 'Do you think they'd miss these if I brought them back to the hotel?'

I shake my head. 'I'll tell them. They'll probably be delighted.'

'Thank you,' he says hoarsely.

'Look, if you want to take them for the day tomorrow, it's OK. If you're not playing golf...'

He looks so earnest when he says, 'I was a fucking idiot. And I'm sorry.'

'What time do you want to pick them up?'

'Tenish?'

'OK.'

'About money, there's plenty in the joint account and I'll be lodging my bonus cheque on Monday.'

I can't deal with this now, so I just nod.

He looks hopeful.

So I need to be clear. 'Ian, just because you're seeing the children doesn't change anything between us. You're still my ex-husband. That won't change.'

'I know.' He bows his head.

'OK.' God, this is so hard.

In bed, I lie awake. Maybe he's telling the truth. Maybe it *is* over. Maybe I don't care. Maybe I do. I shouldn't, though; that's what's important. I need to build a life without him. Tomorrow, I'll have the day to myself. That's where I'll start.

There will be art galleries. Lunch somewhere nice. I will make myself have fun. I will live in the moment. I might even buy a self-help book. Because why the hell not?

Sleep comes with having a purpose and a little more certainty in my life.

thirty-two

Ian arrives on time. The children are bursting to go. He says he'll be back at six and will have them fed. They just about remember to wave goodbye. Off they go, Sam in one arm, Chloe in another. They look so cute, the three of them silhouetted against the morning sun.

The house is suddenly very quiet.

But I have my plans.

Walking into the Orange Gallery is like entering a sanctuary. I amble around in blissful silence, no one pulling out of me, no one asking for anything, no one climbing on something they shouldn't. I inhale the art, actually breathe it in, right into my bones. Time loses relevance.

My favourite art gallery owner makes coffee and we sit together at his desk. I ask about up-and-coming artists. He looks them up on Google Images. It's my ideal day, gazing at new art and arguing over what we like. There isn't much actual argument – Fonsie and I have always been united in our taste. I want ninety per cent of what he hangs in the Orange Gallery, closer to ninety-eight per cent but I'd never admit that to him – we'd have nothing to argue about.

He looks up from his laptop. 'I've missed you.'

I came here every week for twelve years – until I gave up work.

'*I've* missed me,' I joke.

He smiles, no clue what I mean.

'Anyway, I'm back. Every week from now on.'

I ask him about a painting he has hanging. He tells me it's by a new artist he's showing, a man who's recovering from alcoholism and producing great work.

'It's amazing,' I say.

'He's going to be huge. You'll join me for lunch?'

'It's lunch-time already?' I check my watch. 'Wow.'

'You're going to have to eat anyway. May as well join a lonely old man.'

'Less of the "old".' And I hope he's not lonely. Because Fonsie is simply adorable.

We lunch together in a small restaurant a few doors up from the gallery.

'I'm looking for a curator,' he says, peering up over the top of his menu.

'Fonsie, don't. No one has your taste. Seriously. Get a secretary or an accountant or something to handle the business side of things if you're too busy.'

'I think I'll have the soup. It's good here. What are you going for?'

'Probably the Caesar salad,' I say distractedly. 'Fonsie don't let anyone else choose the art.'

'Too late.'

'You've found someone? Have you actually offered the job yet? Because it's not too late…'

He opens out his napkin and places it on his lap.

The waitress takes our order.

'So who is this guy?' I ask with a growing sense of foreboding.

'What makes you think it's a guy? Women have much better taste in art. Of course homosexuals have a wonderful eye too.'

'Who is she?'

'You know her.'

'I do?'

'Let me give you a hint. Young, vivacious, energetic, enthusiastic…'

'Amy Daly?'

'No. She's passionate about art, has exquisite taste, a keen commercial mind…'

'Jane O'Sullivan?'

'That egomaniac?'

I laugh. 'Well then, I don't know. You've got me.'

'She recently packed in a lucrative PR business to write a novel…'

'Oh my God. You're offering me a job?'

'And she's so sharp. Kim, you should see your face.'

'Would you blame me? You've just offered me a job that I've no experience whatsoever for. Besides which, my life is a shambles.'

'Did I just say exquisite taste in art and a keen commercial mind?'

'No art degree, though.'

'A business is a business. And Kim, darling, you've run a business.'

'But PR…'

'I can't imagine anything more relevant, getting publicity for Orange in all the right places, organizing events…'

I stare at him.

'You know, usually it's up to the interviewee to persuade the interviewer. Is this some sort of reverse psychology you're using on me?' He smiles.

'Fonsie, I couldn't.'

'I don't see why not. The children are about to go back to school, aren't they?'

'I'm not sure I'm ready. I'm not sure it's the right time.'

'There's never a right time,' he says, refilling my glass.

'Fonsie, there's a lot of stuff going on in my life.' I look down at the remnants of my Caesar salad and poke an innocent crouton.

'All right. I won't force you. But think about it. I can wait. I want the right person. And I knew who that was the minute she walked through my door this morning. It's fate. And only fools argue with fate. Chin-chin.' He raises his glass.

I smile and clink it. I feel the unfamiliar warm glow that comes with being appreciated.

And then, he has to get back.

'Take your time to think about it, Kim. When you're ready, let me know. I can wait six months at least. If you think you'll be in a better position then to take the job, then great.'

'I'll think about it over the weekend and give you an answer on Monday. And Fonsie? Thank you.'

He winks. 'Don't thank me until you've taken the job.'

At the sink in the hairdresser's, feeling the warm water flow over my scalp, I realise that even though I've forgotten Kim Waters, there are people who haven't. And that makes my tired, flattened heart swell just a little bit.

'Let me do something special today,' Rita says.

'Knock yourself out,' is a lethal instruction to a hairdresser but suddenly I'm feeling reckless.

I close my eyes and imagine that there are no obstacles to Fonsie's offer. I imagine days spent surrounded by what I love, getting to choose what's hung, meeting the artists, giving new talent a break. It's impossible but a girl can dream.

I do a tour of the gallery in my mind, remembering each

painting. I imagine hanging them differently and adding a few more of that new artist. I'm sorry I never asked Fonsie to show me his full portfolio. I will – next time.

'Right, Kim, the moment you've been waiting for.'

I open my eyes, slow to leave this perfect world.

Wow. I turn my head from side to side. It's really good. Maybe even a miracle. Young. Cheeky. A little like pre-Ian Kim.

Passing a flower shop, on impulse, I go in. I'm worth a bunch of lilies. And a bouquet of roses.

I arrive home five minutes before they do.

'Hi, Mum,' Sam and Chloe call, rushing past to get to the TV.

He stands at the door.

I hold it.

'You look great, Kim,' he says.

'I do, don't I?'

'Did you have a good time?'

'Yeah, actually.'

'Good.' He nods. 'Good.'

'I was even offered a job.'

He raises his eyebrows. 'Seriously? What kind?'

'Curator.' Let this lady out for a day and see what happens.

'Of an art gallery?'

I nod.

'Wow. I presume you're going to take it?'

'I'm considering it. Anyway I better get the kids to bed.'

'What about tomorrow?'

I look into his eyes. 'You're not busy?' And we all know what 'busy' is a code for.

'No,' he says firmly. I catch him eyeing the roses. It would never occur to him that I might have bought them for myself. Because I never would have. That was my problem. He looks back at me. 'I could bring them swimming?'

How I wish he'd never stopped. I shrug. 'OK.'

'I'll see you at about twenty-to-ten, then?'

I nod. And close the door.

thirty-three

'Look, Chloe, a fish!' exclaims Sam, clenching his fists and jumping up and down. 'A fish, look, look! It's owange!'

I wondered how long it would take them to notice the surprise I got them, the little distraction.

'Wait – let me see.' On her tiptoes, Chloe peers up at the bowl on the worktop.

'Sit at the table and I'll bring him over.'

Chloe runs to the table. Sam continues to stare at the bowl, following me as though in a trance as I carry it to the table.

'Is it poisonous?' Chloe asks as I sit Sam into his seat.

'No,' I reassure.

'Aw,' Sam says.

'Why didn't you get a poisonous one?' Chloe asks on his behalf.

'They don't sell them.'

'Why not?'

'People don't want to be killed when they're changing the water.'

'Why didn't you get a piranha?'

'Look, I got this little guy because he'd looked lonely. I thought we could be his friends.'

They peer into the bowl. 'OooKay,' they both say together.

'But I'll feed him,' rushes Chloe.

'No, I feed him.'

'No fighting or he goes back to the shop. You can take it in turns. What are you going to call him?'

'Someting scaywee,' says Sam.

'How about Boo?' I suggest.

'Boo!' they shout.

'Careful. Don't frighten him. He's very delicate.'

'What's delicate?'

'Little things frighten him. And when he gets frightened he might have a heart attack or something.'

'What's a hawt attack?'

I explain (somehow) then tell them it's time for bed. Negotiations begin immediately. They end with Sam, Chloe and Boo sleeping in the same room so that Boo won't get lonely and have a heart attack.

'So where did you go today?' I ask, tucking them into the same bed.

'Tara, Mum,' says Chloe.

No. He's supposed to bring them somewhere generic like the zoo. Or McDonald's. Not somewhere special to us – all of us.

Sam sits up. 'Yeah and we fed da hawse. And we wan wit da sheep.' Which means he ran *after* the sheep. 'And we saw'd dogs chasing a wabbit. We'd gweat fun.'

'Did you have a picnic?' Please say no.

He nods enthusiastically.

Apparently, they had gherkins and pickles and salami and olives and rice cakes. Ian remembered everything – all their favourites.

'Oh,' I say, forgetting to hide my disappointment.

'We missed you, Mum,' Chloe says, sitting up.

'I missed you too, sweetie.' My little sensitive soul.

'Why didn't you come?'

'I just had a few things to do. Do you like my hair?'

She nods. 'Will you come the next time?'

'We'll see, honey.' I kiss them both on the forehead. 'Now, go to sleep.'

The house is quiet. I'm restless. I look out at the jungle that is the garden and suddenly I know what to do.

I fly around like a mad thing ripping up, cutting, shredding, snapping. I stuff the results of my blitz into large sacks. Then, I stand observing the result. It's a big improvement. But better than that, I am calm.

I lie down in the grass and gaze up at a sky that is fighting to hold its colour after the sun has left. Swallows scoot and dart through the air, reminding me of Egypt. We couldn't get enough of each other; it seemed a physical impossibility. In seven years, he was always there, could always cheer me up, make me laugh; he always wanted to. Now a wind blows through me. I am hollow.

Bats and stars join the swallows. I watch them until I grow cold.

I go inside.

Hoodie and socks do little to warm me. And though it's still August, I light a fire. I flick on the lamps and curl up on the couch. A dog would be nice.

I gaze at the paintings I've collected over the years, remembering the time I bought each one, where I was, whether I had to save up, borrow or beg, who I was with, if anyone, what I was working at or studying. Each one has its own story. My eyes fall on the one Ian and I bought in Piazza Navona after a particularly liquid lunch. He saw us coming, the artist – giggling and walking a crooked line, in love and in Rome. The painting reminded us of how we'd met – sailing. We couldn't leave it behind.

And I can't stop remembering. I am back to the day we met. On an introduction to sailing course, we were teamed up to right a capsized boat. Into the freezing water we were tipped as the dingy turned on its side. As we struggled to get it back up, it 'turned turtle', flipping over completely. It was Ian who started laughing first. Looking at each other only made us worse. An instructor had to jump in to help us. Success came as our lips turned blue. Sitting in the training boat watching the next couple have a go, the laughter continued. Then, as if by magic, we stopped and looked at each other, knowing that, from that moment on, we would never be apart. We had something. We really had. Never thought it would be so easy to lose.

He comes on time. Takes them swimming. Returns on time. In the afternoon, I try to outdo him by bringing them to a movie. This is what our family has become.

thirty-four

'Does Dad *sleep* in work?' asks Chloe at bedtime.

It would be so easy to lie. But my childhood was one.

'Well, Dad's staying in a hotel at the moment...for a little while.'

She sits up, wide-eyed. 'Does it have a pool? Can I stay too?'

'No, sweetheart.' I tuck a stray strand of hair behind her ear.

'Oh.' She looks down and starts fiddling with the sleeve of her pyjamas. 'Will his holiday be over soon?'

I can answer this. 'Well, hon...' I press her nose gently. 'We'll just have to wait and see.' Is that *it*? We'll *see*? I try again. 'But the good thing is, you're seeing your dad so much now, more than you did when he was sleeping here. Isn't that great?'

She throws me a thunderous look. 'He's Dad. Don't call him "your dad".'

'Sorry. I don't know why I said that. Of course he's Dad. And you do lots of great things with him now, don't you?'

'But why don't *you* come with us?'

'Well, I can get some jobs done.'

'I can help with the jobs,' she says hopefully.

Heart breaking here. 'Thanks, sweetie. We'll see.'

Her thumb slips into her mouth. A little frown appears. Something else is brewing. Now would be a good time to bolt.

'You still love Dad, don't you, Mum?'

I look at her little face and see him in it, so much of him. It is like being forced to face a truth I've been denying myself. Of course I love him. It wouldn't hurt so much if I didn't.

'Yes, Chloe. I still love your dad, I mean Dad.' That doesn't mean I don't hate him too. Because I do.

'And Dad loves you, Mum.'

What can I say – no he doesn't or he wouldn't have done what he did? My alternative is, 'I know sweetie. Come on, let's snuggle.'

I lie beside her until she sleeps.

And that is how I end up back at the psychologist. I don't know what else to do. And I have to do something.

Weird thing is, I find myself talking about my parents. Specifically, The Deal.

'How does that make you feel about your father?' he asks so calmly – like he's seen it all in here, in his 1970's office.

I shrug.

He waits.

'I don't know. Like he was an illusion? And he made our lives one?'

'Do you hate him for that?'

I grimace. 'Isn't hate a bit strong?'

'Are you angry with him?'

'Yes, I'm angry. Of course, I'm angry. Especially at how he treated Mum.'

'What about how he treated you?'

I shrug. 'You cheat on your wife, you cheat on your family.'

'But you can't hate a dead man, is that it?'

'I'm just going to have to accept it, right? Otherwise everything Mum has sacrificed will have been for nothing.'

'You're allowed to feel, Kim. In fact, you should. It's healthy.'

'So, it's OK to hate him?' I ask doubtfully.

'It's OK to be honest with yourself. When someone we love dies, it's natural to remember only the good in them. No one is all good.'

That is when I realise: I made him a better father than any other. I canonised him.

'I've a suggestion and I want you to think before you answer.'

I look at him warily.

'I'd like Ian to attend your next session.'

I tense. '*Why?*'

'To help you understand what happened to your marriage so you can move forward.'

'He'll make it my fault. And I've had too much of that. Anyway, it doesn't matter why. He did what he did.'

'Sometimes, to move forward, we have to look back.'

'He wouldn't come anyway.'

'If he doesn't want to, we'll manage. But we'll manage better and make more progress if he does. You deserve this, Kim. Why don't you ask him, see if he'll come?'

I hesitate. 'He'll think I want us back together!'

'Then be clear about that with him. Tell him why he's coming – for you.'

I sigh. 'OK.'

Later, Ian phones.

'How are you?' he asks.

'Spectacular.'

Awkward pause.

'Kim, can I come over? There's something I want to ask you.'

'Ask now.' He can't just come over anytime he likes.

He clears his throat. 'Right. OK. Um. Chloe tells me next Tuesday is her first day at big school.'

'Yeah.'

'Would you mind if I came along? I'd love to be there. I could take the morning off.'

'It would be an hour of your time. Not a morning.'

'So it's OK then?'

'You know she'd love you there.'

'And you?'

'It's not my day.'

'I know. Thanks, though. I appreciate it.'

I take a deep breath. 'I'm going to a psychologist. He thinks it'd be good for my "progress" for you to come to my next session. I told him it would be a waste of time…'

'I'll come.' His voice sounds crumbly. 'I wish I'd gone when you first suggested it.'

'This is not to get back together. It's so I can move forward. You need to be clear about that.'

'I am. But I'd like a chance to say sorry. Officially.'

'As long as you're not expecting anything.'

'I'm not.'

'It's just for one session. Then I can get on with it on my own.'

'OK. Thanks.'

'I don't know why you're thanking me.'

'I don't either,' he tries to joke.

I give him the date and time. 'It's OK if it doesn't suit.'

'It suits. It's fine. I'll see you then.'

thirty-five

Ian is in the waiting room when I arrive. He looks as nervous as I feel. I want to cry. For all we have lost.

He stands. 'Hey.'

'Hey.'

We sit at exactly the same time.

He smiles.

Mine is a reflex. I remind myself to be on my guard in future.

Apart from us, the waiting room's empty.

I check my watch. 'I usually don't have to wait long.'

'It's fine. It's good to get out of the office.'

I think of her. And want to punch him.

The door opens and we're called in.

They shake hands.

'Thanks for coming, Ian. I think it'll be useful.'

We take our seats when really I want to run.

He asks us about our marriage.

Ian talks about how great it was.

I say nothing.

'We used to be a team. Did everything together.' He looks at me. 'We were best friends. Soulmates.'

'And you threw it away,' I say because – enough. Seriously.

Ian looks at Peter.

'Did things start to go wrong before you had the affair?' he asks Ian.

Ian nods. 'When Kim gave up work, it changed. It's like it wasn't the two of us against the world any more.' He turns to me. 'It was like you and the kids against me.'

I shake my head. I *knew* this would be a mistake.

'I'm just trying to explain,' he says to me. 'You resented me getting out of the house even though I was just going to work. Maybe *I'd* have liked to quit. Maybe *I'd* have liked to explore my artistic side, start over, become a writer. But someone had to put bread on the table. I'm not complaining. I'm just saying that you weren't the only one under pressure. Yes, I was going out the door but I was doing so worried about the mortgage and who'd pay it if I wasn't kept on. I would have liked for you to understand that it wasn't just hard on you. Instead, I felt I was being blamed for everything.'

'For what, Ian?'

'For not doing enough housework. For you having a shitty day. For example.'

I stare at him. 'I wasn't *blaming* you for my day – I just needed to get out of the house. It's not easy being responsible for toddlers every hour of every day. And why shouldn't I ask for help when I'm trying to juggle everything on my own?'

'I didn't ask you to take on all that stuff.'

'Who else was going to do it? Certainly not you. And not an au pair.'

'You felt under pressure, Kim. Is that right?' Peter asks.

I look at Ian. 'I wish you'd just taken me away for a weekend. We could've been alone together. We needed it – so badly. But no. No weekends until she came along – then lots of weekends – for you and her. You tried very hard to save our marriage, Ian.'

'What about your weekend with Connor? If you hadn't gone, I wouldn't have ended up away from home feeling lost, alone, worried... I wouldn't have...' He stops.

As does my heart. So *that's* when it started.

'You always got on better with Connor than me.'

'That's your perception. And don't blame me because of how you feel about Connor. I didn't have an affair with him.' I remember our fling then remind myself that it was over with Ian by then. I will not feel guilty.

'But why did you have to go away when I specifically asked you not to?' Ian asks, desperately. 'Why?'

'Oh my God. You don't remember, do you? You were being obnoxious – you were The Man Who Needed The Exact Number Of Sausages At Exactly The Right Time. You were constantly putting me down and pushing me away. I had to get away. Connor wanted us to come. You didn't seem to want us at all.'

'It's the other way around. You didn't want me. I'd get in from work and you'd be out the door. You didn't care about my day, never asked, weren't interested.'

'I was *tired.*'

'I asked you not to go to London.'

'Because of how little *you* think of Connor. Not a good enough reason. Anyway you were going to be away yourself.'

'So the affair began that weekend?' Peter asks.

Ian looks at him. 'It hurt that she wouldn't listen, didn't care, wouldn't see... Connor has always fancied her. I was miserable, got drunk. Jackie was there.'

'And then you came home and accused *me* of having an affair. What kind of person does that?'

He drops his head. 'A guilty one.'

'You made me out to be the bad guy so you'd feel better? Low, Ian.'

'Not deliberately. I don't know; everything was upside down, out of control, mad.'

'I still don't know which is worse – the fact you cheated and lied or that you treated me like a fool. All those put downs, those references to my figure, what I wore…. You even wondered what I could possibly write about apart from cellulite.'

He looks baffled. 'If you say I said those things, then I must have. But I never set out to hurt you. I might have been worried for you, not wanting you to turn into something you never wanted to be. I was worried that you'd end up unhappy. But you're right; I was out of line. I'm sorry. Sorry for everything.' He bows his head. 'I was insecure and stupid. A bloody fool.' He looks at me. 'But I love you, Kim, more than anything. If you would just give me a chance to make it up to you…'

'To trample all over me, you mean. I'm starting to remember who I am. I'm starting to *like* who I am.'

'I love who you are.'

I look at him. 'But how easily you forgot.'

'Well, I think we've made good progress here today,' Peter says, looking at the clock.

Progress? It feels as if something that was beginning to settle has been stirred up and swirled around like grime at the bottom of a lake.

'I could come again if you think it would help,' Ian suggests.

Peter glances from Ian to me. 'You might like to decide that together.'

Ian looks at me hopefully.

I get up and leave.

Outside, Ian catches up with me. He touches my arm. 'Kim…'

I pull away and look into his eyes. 'You could have had a bit of faith in me. In us. You could have tried, Ian. Instead of falling so easily into her arms.' I turn and go before I break down in front of him.

How can *that* have been progress?

thirty-six

I go to collect the children from Mum's. They're out the back, chasing each other with plastic watering cans. Their innocence breaks my heart.

We stand watching them.

'Have you given up on the hose?' I ask Mum.

'Well, they're supposed to be watering the plants.'

I smile. 'Were they OK?'

'Wonderful. They love to potter around together, don't they?'

You see? I'm not the only one.

'Coffee?' Mum asks.

'I'm not staying,' for five hundred questions.

'Did you make any progress?'

'No.'

'Did he explain?'

'Can we not talk about this?'

'He *has* ended the affair, though?'

'How do I know? His word means nothing.' *He* means nothing.

'Is he sorry?'

'Mum. What did I just say about his word?'

'But does he still want to come back?'

'Enough, OK? I'm not you. I deal with things differently. It *is* allowed.'

'You have to think of the children. It's not just about you.'

I am not a bad mother. I am *not* a bad mother. I hurry across the grass and retrieve my soaked children, becoming drenched myself in the process. They're disappointed at my lack of reaction.

'Come on, guys, we're going home.'

Somehow, they know not to argue.

Unfortunately, we have to get out through the house.

'Say goodbye to Granny.'

They run to hug her. Which is when I realise how much better they know her now. They have a relationship.

I soften. 'Thanks for minding them.'

'Anytime. Bye, love. Sorry for nagging, it's just that...'

'Mum!'

'OK. OK. Sorry.' She puts her hands up.

'I'll see you soon.'

I feed the kids, skip their bath and get them to bed early. I'm crawling into my own bed when the phone rings.

'Have you been avoiding me?' Connor asks.

'Sorry?'

'You never called me back.'

'Didn't I?' I can't remember a call where I promised I would.

'What about the message I left? Didn't that remind you?'

I remember now. 'Sorry. I meant to get back to you.'

'Not like you to forget.'

'I'm having a few problems, Connor. I *think* I can be forgiven for not returning a phone call.' Jesus.

'Sorry.' A beat. 'How are you?'

'Fine.'

'I keep thinking about you.'

'Yeah, well I'm grand. Still seeing the shrink,' I joke.

'What's the story with Ian?'

I fight the urge to hang up. 'He's seeing the children.'

'How often?'

'I don't know, most days.'

'Is that wise?'

'Who knows *what's* wise? Everyone but me it seems.'

'What's wrong?'

'Nothing.'

'It's just that it might be better if you didn't see him so much. You need a clean break.'

'Connor, I would love nothing more than a clean break. He's the children's father. What they need matters. I'm not going to be selfish about this.'

'Just don't be fooled by him. He's probably still sleeping with her.'

'Despite appearances, I'm not a complete eejit. I can look after myself. OK?'

'OK.' There's a silence. 'It's just that I care about you. I care what happens to you.'

'Well don't. You've your life. And you've Sarah. She's thrilled to have you back.'

'I know. I'm lucky.'

'So sound it. Thanks for calling, Connor, but I need to do this my own way, OK?'

'OK. Goodnight, then. Talk to you tomorrow.'

'No. I'm fine.'

'I'd like to check up on you. Make sure you're OK.'

'I *am* OK. I have to sort this out for myself – without discussing everything I think and feel, OK?'

Silence. Then: 'OK.'

'Is Sarah there? Can I've a quick word?'

'No, she's out. As usual. Goodnight, Kim. Take care.'

I collapse onto the bed and put the phone on silent.

thirty-seven

Chloe's first day at school and Ian arrives at 8.20. Having him in the kitchen first thing, dressed for work, reminds me of how life used to be. Except for one thing. He no longer looks at home, standing awkwardly inside the kitchen door, arms folded. I'm swallowing back Solpadeine for a headache.

'Our little girl is growing up,' he says, smiling over at her.

'Look at my uniform, Dad.' She jumps down from the table and performs an amateur but heart-warming twirl. Her delight at Ian being here for her special day is obvious.

'Wow,' he says. 'Look at you.'

I glance at Sam who is, after forty minutes, finally finishing his one Weetabix. He is unusually quiet. I kiss the top of his head so he's not feeling left out.

'My man,' I say to him. It's the same innocent term of endearment I've used since he was a baby but suddenly it takes on a new significance, as if I'm sending a message to Ian that he isn't my man any more.

'Back in a sec,' says Ian, disappearing out the door.

He returns with presents – a new suspension bridge for one of Sam's train sets and a pair of Barbie roller skates for Chloe. I haven't bought them anything. Damn.

'Nifty,' says our almost five-year-old and I can't help smiling.

The doorbell rings. Chloe rushes out ahead of me.

It's Mum, arriving unexpectedly. Am I the only one not to have bought presents? Chloe drops to the floor and starts to rip off the wrapping paper. Then she is flinging herself at her granny in gratitude.

'Have a wonderful day, pet,' Mum says, a little teary.

'Thanks Gran and thanks for the paints.'

'You're welcome, sweetheart. I've a little something for Sam, too.'

'He's in the kitchen,' Chloe says, sitting back on the ground with her first proper paint set.

'Oh! Ian!' Mum says on reaching the kitchen. She turns to me with a big smile and sparkly eyes, then goes to give him a hug. 'It's good to see you. How are you?'

Traitor.

'I'm fine, Florence, thank you. How are you?' He pats her back affectionately. Ian always did love Mum.

'Oh, Ian, I'm well.'

Then comes an awkward moment. Where does the conversation go now?

Sam saves the day. He, too, loves his present, a kaleidoscope.

Chloe arrives to check it out.

'Well, love, I'll get going,' Mum says to me. 'Just wanted to wish Chloe luck.'

'Aren't you coming with us to the school?' I ask.

'No. I've got to…. rush off.'

'OK, well, thanks so much for the pressies. You know how Chloe loves art.'

'Like her mother.' She smiles, then goes over to Chloe, stoops down and kisses her. 'Have a great day. Have fun.'

'Bye Gran and thanks for the paints. They're great.'

'And tanks for my kliidascope. It's bwill.'

She ruffles his hair. 'Bye, gorgeous.'

And then she's gone. Leaving more awkwardness. How do we get to the school – all together or separately? For obvious reasons, I'd prefer separately. But maybe this can be my present to Chloe.

'You may as well come with us, I suppose,' I say to Ian.

His eyes say, 'thank you.'

Mine say, 'I'm not doing this for you.'

We drop Sam at the Montessori. He puts up a fight because he's used to his sister going in with him. I promise a train ride. And have to shake on it before he'll budge.

We drive to the school, Ian making small talk with Chloe.

As we're about to go in, Ian starts taking photos. He takes a few shots of Chloe, more with Chloe and a friend from the Montessori, then one of Chloe and me.

'Let me take one of the family,' says a passing Good Samaritan.

'No thanks; it's OK,' I rush.

'Thank you; that'd be great,' Ian says, at the same time.

We look at each other. She looks at us.

Then I see Chloe's face.

'Sorry. Thank you. That would be lovely,' I say.

We squat behind our daughter and smile. I think of the photo of my father with James and me and am ambushed by a range of emotions, none of them good.

Cheese!

As I drive him back to the house to get his car, I feel his gaze on me.

'I miss you. I miss our life,' he says.

I keep my eyes on the road. There's no point having this conversation.

'We haven't spoken about money,' he says.

'No.'

'What if I just keep my salary going into the joint account?'

'OK.'

'I'm changing firm but there won't be a problem with the account. It's all set up. But if there *is* a problem of any sort, just let me know and I'll sort it.'

'So you're leaving?' I confirm looking straight ahead. Does this mean he really has left her? Do I care? Unfortunately, the answer is yes. But I'll work on that.

'Yeah. At the end of the month.' He sighs deeply. 'I'd been trying to for a while. Kim, I know you'll find this hard to believe but I hated what I was doing. I hated myself. I wanted to end it. I thought that if I got another job, it would be easier. I received an offer just before going into that board meeting. I'd handed in my notice and ended the affair before you arrived.'

'How did she take the news?' I ask coldly.

'I meant nothing to her. I was a distraction.'

I think of a cat toying with a mouse. Two mice, though. Because she toyed with my life too. Ruined it, actually. So, four mice. Because… the kids.

I pull up outside the house. Suddenly I have to know. I turn to him, look right into his eyes.

'Did you love her?'

'No,' he says simply. 'It was never about love. I was lonely.' He looks at me. 'I only love you. I've only ever loved you. I can't believe that it has taken this to make me realise how great you are, how great my life was.' His voice breaks and he starts to cry. 'I'm sorry, Kim.'

I get out of the car. Go inside.

I pace the back garden, trying to empty my mind. Connor was right. A clean break would be so much easier. The phone bleeps. It's a text from Connor wondering how I'm doing. Doesn't he listen? Doesn't he know when to leave a person alone? I switch the phone to silent and go back into the house. I start to clear up after breakfast. Wiping the counter, I knock into the lilies. Great clumps of pollen rain down on the fish bowl.

'Oh God. Don't eat it, Boo, please don't eat it!' The last thing we need is a dead goldfish.

I swipe the vase away then race to the drawer for a spoon. When I get back to the bowl Boo is at the surface, gulping great big fishy mouthfuls of bright yellow pollen. Oh, sweet Jesus. I scoop out what's left, then ring the pet shop.

'Hi, it's me again.' I've been on a bit.

'Hi, Kim.'

'Is pollen poisonous to fish?'

'Gosh, that's a new one on me. Couldn't tell you.'

'He's just eaten a load of it.'

'What type?'

'Lilies.'

'Hmmm.'

'Is that bad?'

'Haven't a clue.'

'What should I do?'

'I'd probably change the water. And... try not to worry.' OK, so the guy's laughing at me. He has to get his kicks somehow.

I do as recommended. Then peer into the bowl. Boo *looks* OK. I wonder when we're out of the woods.

Rather than watch a life-or-death struggle, I head for town. There's a gallery owner who needs an answer.

In trying to explain my 'no' to Fonsie, it all comes out. Well not all. But most.

'The children have lost their father and don't even know it. I need to be there for them.'

'Sounds to me like you need a diversion,' he says calmly.

I shake my head. 'The children need stability, Fonsie.' You can always tell the people seeing shrinks – they use words like stability.

'What about part-time? You could still be there for the children and have a distraction from everything else. It could be your sanctuary.'

I smile at his use of the word. A sanctuary is exactly what it would be. And there's the money – whatever he offers, it would be a step towards independence. But: 'What kind of hours were you thinking?'

'How does three hours a day, four days a week sound?'

I squint at him. 'Would that be enough for you?'

'It would be perfect.'

I could still drop the kids off and pick them up. It wouldn't make a difference to them – apart from having a happier mum who'd have enjoyed her morning instead of wasting time trying to do the impossible – may as well admit it, Kim Waters is no novelist. I take a deep breath. It's a relief to admit it.

'So when would you like to start?' he asks.

I love him for his persistence.

'How often does a chance like this come along?' he persists further.

'Never.'

'Why don't you take a few weeks to allow the children settle into school? I want to start paying you from today though, so you won't change your mind.'

'Fonsie, there's no need. I'll take the job. Starting next week.'

'Excellent.' He shoots out his hand. 'Shake.'

I laugh. Suddenly this feels so right. 'You have no idea how much this means to me.'

'Ditto, kid.'

thirty-eight

On my way home, I call in to Mum to share the news.

She sweeps me into a hug. Then she pulls back abruptly.

'You'll need new outfits!'

'Damn. I hadn't thought of that.'

'My treat.'

'No!'

'Yes!' She grows serious. 'It's my way of saying sorry. You were right, Kim. We *are* different people and you must do what's right for you. I'm sorry for not seeing that. I'm sorry for putting the children before you.' She starts to get emotional. 'We shouldn't argue. I'm going to stop nagging. I promise.'

'Good.' I smile.

'Let's have a glass of sherry to celebrate.'

'Ooooh. Sherry before noon? That Charles is a bad influence.'

She giggles then produces the goods.

We sit on the patio and toast Fonsie. The sun breaks through.

I put my face to it. It feels like it's warming my bones, right through to the marrow.

'I shouldn't have told you about Dad when you had so much on your plate. I wanted to show you another way.'

'It's OK,' I say to cut her off.

'And I'm sorry I hid it from you all this time; I wanted you to go on adoring him the way you always have.'

I turn from the sun to look at her. 'I'm glad you told me. I don't want to be under any illusions. Ever again.'

She reaches out and grips my hand. 'I'm sorry for saying you always put yourself first. It's simply not true.' She is starting to tear up.

'Mum. Forget it. Seriously.'

'I can't. You're great.'

'Please don't cry. You were right to tell me. And you were right to do what you did – with Dad. I'm getting used to the idea, really I am.' OK, so that's a lie.

'I was so happy to see Ian in the kitchen,' she says dabbing her eyes and giving her nose a quick honk. 'Did you see how much it meant to Chloe that he was there?'

I just nod.

'And it wasn't *so* bad for you, was it?'

'I've told him that he can see the children as much as he likes. So far, it's going OK.'

'Oh, that's marvellous.'

I give her a look.

'I'll keep my nose out of it. I promise. So...' She claps her hands. 'How are the newly-weds? I'm still in shock.'

'You're not the only one.'

'I'm glad Connor has settled down, though. I used to think he liked you. I sometimes wondered if Ian picked up on it.'

Will she continue to surprise me for the rest of my life?

'They're fine, as far as I know,' I manage.

'Anyway, it's good that they've found each other.'

'Yeah.'

One week later, on a warm September day, I become an official employee. I underestimated how good it would feel to dress up and go into town, to have a purpose of my own, a world of my own and to have my opinion sought, listened to, acted on.

We move things around. Contact the new artist I like and arrange for him to bring in more of his work. Hours pass like seconds. I ask Fonsie if he'd like me to work on a PR proposal for Orange.

'Absolutely.'

'First we'd have to sit down and go through the gallery's strengths and weaknesses as well as the opportunities and threats that are out there. We'd look at target audiences and what you want to say.'

'*We* want to say.'

I smile.

'Let's start now. I'll make the coffee.'

I leave Orange on a high, my mind buzzing with ideas. I'm almost at the school when, stopped at lights, I remember to turn on my phone. There are messages from Connor, Sarah, Ian and the school all asking me to call them. It's the one from the school I worry about.

I hurry into the yard. The bell has just gone and the children are coming out. I see Chloe, all in one piece and smiling. I breathe again.

'Everything all right?' I ask.

'Yep, have you got my drink?'

I hand it to her. 'Did anything happen today?'

'A boy had a nosebleed. It was *disgusting*.'

'OK, we have to go inside for a minute.' I take her hand.

Chloe brings me to her classroom where her teacher is tidying up.

I introduce myself. We shake hands.

'Is everything OK?' I ask.

'Yes, yes, nothing urgent. The principal would like a word.'

'The *principal*?'

She smiles. 'It's nothing serious; she just wants a chat.'

Chats are always serious.

'I'll just pop in and see if she's free. Would you mind holding on here for a minute?'

'Well, I have to collect my son....'

'Won't be long.'

I smile down at Chloe.

'What does she want?' she asks.

'Just a chat.'

'About what?'

'School probably.'

And that is a good enough answer for a four-year-old.

The teacher is back. And smiling. 'Ms Dempsey will see you now. Chloe why don't you stay here with me? You can do some colouring while I tidy up.'

Chloe and I look at each other, neither of us wanting to separate. What do they have to say that she can't hear?

I wink at her. 'See you in a minute, dude. Dying to see what you draw.'

'It's just colouring in,' she says glumly.

'So use good colours.' I smile brightly. 'Back in a sec.'

The blonde, leopard-skin-clad principal, (yes, really), introduces herself and tells me to take a seat. Then she gets straight to the point.

'Mrs Kavanagh, Chloe has head lice.'

A few instant reactions:

One: I am *not* Mrs Kavanagh.

Two: my daughter does not have head lice; it must be a mistake.

My third reaction is the one I stick with: Yuck.

'Are you sure? I wash her hair very regularly.'

'But do you check it regularly?'

'Sorry?'

'Do you fine-comb it, once a week?'

'Well, not lately,' meaning, not ever. 'But I will of course from now on. And I'll take her to buy a lotion immediately.'

'She must have had them for quite a while for us to notice them. We don't take it upon ourselves to hunt for head lice. We leave it up to the parents.'

Christ.

'But in Chloe's case, well, they were pretty obvious.'

How didn't I see them? Someone point me in the direction of the nearest hole so I can crawl in.

'Sorry. I'm stunned. Thank you for letting me know. I'll take care of it.'

'Is everything all right on the home front?' she asks cheerily.

Who the hell does she think she is? 'Everything's fine.'

'It's not just the lice, you see. Chloe seems withdrawn. Preoccupied. Lost in her own thoughts. She doesn't concentrate in class...'

'She's just started school. Surely there's an adjustment period?'

'Absolutely. That could be it. Just thought I'd mention it seeing as I had you here. It might be an idea to discuss things with her, see how she feels about starting school, that kind of thing.'

'I will. Thank you for bringing this to my attention.' I stand up. Because: enough.

'Super.' She stands and shakes my hand. Another parent dealt with.

I walk up the corridor feeling like a child again, having been sent to the principal. Am I neglecting my children? Maybe I haven't been listening, noticing things I should have. Maybe I shouldn't have taken the job.

'I *love* it,' I say when I see Chloe's page of colour and complete disregard for the lines. I pick her up and hold her close. 'Let's go, sweetie.'

We rush to collect Sam. Then it's straight to the pharmacy for the most powerful head-lice lotion on the market. I get two bottles, just in case. Everyone's getting a dose.

As soon as we're home, I run the bath, fill it with toys – and two children.

When I smell the stuff, I know I won't get away with clandestine dosing. So a new game, 'zapping the enemy', is invented.

After the bath, one by one, I sit them by the window and go through their hair with the special comb. Oh. My. God. These have to be the ugliest, most grotesque creatures in existence. And they both have them.

'Can I be finished now, Mum?' Chloe asks as I slide a nit off a hair.

'No pet. We gotta get these guys out. They're tough. But we're tougher.'

'K.'

God, my hair is so itchy. I feel like I'm crawling.

As soon as the kids are done, I cover my head in the stuff and wait for it to do its magic. Eyes smarting from the fumes, I wonder who else needs treatment. Mum. And Ian. There's a strong temptation to let Ian harvest a crop. The only problem is, he'd spread them back to the kids.

With Sam occupied with an episode of *Thomas The Tank Engine*, I suggest to Chloe that we draw for a while, real pictures, not colouring in. I'm hoping that, while we work, she might open up.

We're almost finished our pictures – of head lice – when she finally starts to talk.

'Did Dad go away 'cause I was bold?' she asks, without looking up from her picture.

'No, sweetheart, of course not. Anyway, you're not bold. You're a very good girl.'

She looks up. 'Was it because I was fighting with Sam?'

'No! It has absolutely nothing to do with you or Sam.'

'Mum, Dad doesn't love me any more.'

'Yes, he does! *Of course* he does. Come here.'

I pop her up on my lap and stroke her cheek with my finger. 'He loves you so, so much. And I love you. We both love you.'

'Then why doesn't he come home?'

'He comes to see you every day.'

'But he doesn't come to see you.'

'It's just that I'm very busy at the moment.'

She stares straight into my eyes, right in, right to the back. 'Why don't you smile any more, Mum?'

'I do. See?'

'I mean a real one. And what's wrong with your voice?'

'Nothing.'

'It's sad. All the time.'

Is it? Jesus. 'I'm sorry. I didn't mean it to be. I'm not sad. Will I tell you a joke?'

'No.' She usually loves my jokes. And I love hers – mainly because they're not funny, which makes them hilarious.

'I'm sorry, Chloe. I'll be more fun, I promise.'

'Will you laugh?'

'Definitely.'

'Will you play with us?'

'Don't I?'

'Not anymore.'

'I'm sorry. I didn't realise.'

'Will you do family things with us when Dad comes?'

God. 'We'll see.'

She gives me that look again.

'If I'm not busy, OK?'

'Don't be busy, Mum.'

'Thomas is over,' says Sam, padding into the kitchen in the cutest bare feet in the world. 'Will you remind it?'

I will never correct him on remind and rewind. Never.

'I've a better idea,' I say. 'Why don't we have some ice cream and a game of chasing?'

Chloe drops her crayon. 'Yaay!'

'And I was thinking,' I say to her. 'Would you like to invite any new friends from school to play?' Lice-free ones, preferably.

'That's a great idea,' she says. 'Let me think about who.'

'Take your time. You don't have to come up with someone straight away. Maybe decide when you're in school tomorrow.'

'OK!'

We sit on a rug in the back garden, having an ice cream picnic.

'What does "my heart's bruised" mean?' asks Chloe.

'Where did you hear that?' I ask, alarmed.

'It's in that song. You know. The one we like.'

'"Out of Reach"?'

She nods.

'OK. My heart's bruised means, well; sometimes when people are talking about love they talk about their heart being in love. And the girl in the song is saying that her heart is bruised because her boyfriend has just gone off with another girl and she's upset about it.'

'Oh.' She's quiet for a moment and then says, 'He should have told her, shouldn't he?'

'He should have told her what?'

'That he was going off with the other girl. Then it would have been OK, wouldn't it?'

'Well, no.'

'Why not? They could have all gone off together.'

'I don't think that would have worked.'

'Why? It's OK for two girls to love the same boy, isn't it?'

'I *suppose* it's OK but the boy should decide between the girls.'

'Why?'

Chloe should be having this conversation with her granny because suddenly, I no longer have the answers. 'It's just the way it is.'

thirty-nine

Connor calls before I can return his text.

'How are things?'

'Great,' I reassure him – because clearly he needs it. 'I'm a workingwoman, curator of the gallery you bought Modigliani man in. Any day now I'll be able to buy him back from you.'

'Do you think you can manage a job right now?'

'*Hello?* Is this the person who imagined me *running* a gallery?'

'That was before. What about the kids?'

'It's part-time. Doesn't affect them.'

'You shouldn't have to work.'

'I *want* to.'

'You need someone to look after you.'

'That is the very *last* thing I need. I *love* being independent again.'

'I'd like to look after you.'

'What?'

'I can't stop thinking of you, of us…. We're meant to be together, Kim.'

'Jesus, Connor. What is *wrong* with you?'

'I love you.'

'Well, snap out of it! You're married. And you're lucky – Sarah's great.'

'Sarah was a mistake. It's you I love. It's you I want.'

If it were anyone else, I'd hang up. 'That's never going to happen.'

'It could. You're free. I could divorce Sarah.'

'I would *hate* you for doing that. Anyway, I don't love you. I'm sorry. But I don't.'

'You still love him? After what he's done? After what happened between us?'

'What happened was a mistake. And you know it.'

'No I don't.'

'I'm hanging up, Connor.' I do, then throw the phone onto the couch like it's infected.

It starts to ring. I stare at it, heart pounding. What did I do to encourage him? *What?* Well, the sex obviously. I should have stopped it. Not been so weak. So bloody needy. God.

It rings out, then starts again. Cursing, I turn it on silent.

Out in the garden, I yank the lawnmower out of the shed. At least my pacing will be productive.

I inhale the smell of freshly cut grass and grow marginally optimistic. He knows I don't want to be with him now. I've made that clear. I was firm. It'll be fine.

Ian returns from McDonald's with the children.

'Here, I'll do that,' he says.

'It's OK. I'm done.'

'Let me at least put away the lawnmower.'

'I've got it!'

He looks at me strangely.

I look straight back at him. I don't need his help.

He puts the kids to bed. His storytelling voice floats down the stairs. And I wish – so hard – that he had done this before and that there wasn't a reason behind it now.

When he finally comes down, I tell him about the lice.

'OK,' he says, like he's not panicking. 'How would I know if I had them?'

'You'd be itchy.'

He scratches his head. 'Shit.'

I smile, get up, go to the bathroom and retrieve the comb. 'You need to get someone to check your hair with one of these.'

He looks at it like it's an actual louse. 'Where'll I get one?'

'Pharmacy.'

He looks at me. 'Would *you* check me?'

I raise a cold eyebrow.

'Who else can I ask?'

'Do I really have to remind you?'

He sighs deeply. 'When are you going to start believing me? It's over.' It's the way he says it, as though exhausted, exasperated, fed up with it all.

And, finally, I believe him.

'OK. I'll do it,' I say. 'On one condition.'

He looks at me.

'You do mine.'

'Deal.'

I go first and talk him through it so he can reciprocate. I part his hair and check his scalp. Over and over. Even if he were still seeing her, he'd never ask her to do this. This is the kind of job for a wife. A mistress is only ever shown the best version of you. The sanitized, sexy, witty you.

'You're OK,' I say, stepping back.

'Phew!' He stands up. Then gestures to the seat flamboyantly. 'Madame.'

I sit down.

I never thought I would let him touch me again. And here he is, methodically parting my hair, like a chimpanzee grooming his mate.

'Oh oh,' he says after a few minutes, just when I was beginning to hope I was OK.

'Oh shit. Have you found one?' I shiver automatically.

'What colour did you say they were?' he asks carefully, his fingers on pause.

'Browny-grey. Have you found one?'

'Actually, no.' He points at me. 'Got you, though.'

His laughter is a reminder of what we had. Once.

'You'd better keep going,' I say flatly.

He carries on in silence.

I hear his breathing – loud and through his mouth, as always when he's concentrating. Something else hasn't changed – his smell – so familiar, so Iany. No more aftershave, then.

He rubs the top of my hair and taps my shoulders. 'All done.'

I stand up. 'Thanks.'

'Kim?'

'You should probably go now.'

He nods. 'Yeah.'

I close the front door behind him and lean against it, my hollow heart aching. Safe now to cry.

I lock up and go get my phone. It vibrates in my hand. When I see who it is, I explode. Right! Enough!

'Connor, what do you want?'

'Why did you hang up on me?'

'Why do you think? You weren't listening. I don't love you. And Sarah is my friend.'

'But that night must have meant something...'

'Well it didn't, OK? If you call me again as a friend I'll be happy to talk but if you even *mention* the other thing, that's the end of our friendship. We go back a long time, Connor. But enough is enough.'

'We're meant to be together.'

I hang up.

This time he doesn't call back.

I go upstairs. What is *wrong* with him? I wrap my arms around myself and go check on the kids.

I sit on Chloe's bed gazing at her little face, soft and relaxed, her hand curled up but fingers loose. It doesn't seem like five years since Ian, his hand on my tummy, sang rebel songs to the tiny person she was becoming. I told him that the baby would be born a rebel. He smiled and said, 'like her Mum'. Feels like such a long time ago.

I touch Sam's flushed cheek with the backs of my fingers and smile remembering the names I genuinely considered for him when I was pregnant. Cosmo. Denzel. Frodo. Ian didn't dismiss any. He said nothing until Sam was born, then simply asked, 'How about Sam?' I looked down at his tiny wrinkly face and saw that he was Sam. Samuel Denzel Kavanagh.

'I love you,' I whisper.

I kiss him gently on the forehead and head to bed, a bed that seems incredibly large tonight.

In my next therapy session, Peter asks if I've managed to put the Connor incident behind me. I hesitate. Because Connor goes to him too. But there's no one else I can ask.

'Actually, I'm a bit worried….' I tell him about the phone calls.

He takes it seriously. Which is good (I'm not paranoid) and bad (there *is* something to worry about).

'I should talk to him,' he says.

'Don't tell him I told you.'

'What you and I speak about is between us, Kim. And what I discuss with Connor will have to be the same. I'll just call him to check progress and take it from there.'

'Thank you.' I feel my shoulders fall in relief.

'If he calls you with the same intention, don't talk to him.

Hang up. That's important. Let me talk to him, hmm? And don't worry. I'll see you next week.'

There are three messages from Connor when I switch my phone back on after work the following day, all of them going over old ground, his voice growing increasingly frustrated. Remembering Peter's advice, I turn off my phone and try to stay calm as I go to pick up the children.

We go to the park. And I try to put it from my mind.

When we get home, Chloe tells me there are messages on the answering machine.

'I'll get them later,' I say cheerfully.

She insists.

So do I.

Ian arrives. 'You've messages,' he says passing the answering machine.

'She said she'll get them later,' Chloe says. Then shrugs like I'm weird.

'Busy,' I explain.

'Want me to rewind them for you?' he asks.

'No!' I bark.

He looks at me strangely.

'I'll get them later,' I say calmly.

The phone rings. I swivel in shock. If I don't pick up, the machine will click on and everyone will hear.

'You go on into the kitchen,' I say lightly.

I run to the phone, pick it up, listen, then drop the receiver.

I delete the messages and take the phone off the hook. Just to be on the safe side, I plug the phone and answering machine out altogether.

Heart pounding, I go back to the kitchen. When is he going to stop? What do I have to do? What do I have to say?

The kids are out the back. Ian is standing at the door, arms folded, watching them. He turns. Then squints at me.

'You OK?'

I nod, not trusting myself to speak. I busy myself making coffee, which in itself is suspicious – me making him coffee – but if I don't do something I'll lose it.

'You *would* tell me if there was something wrong?'

I nod again, unable to say, 'I don't need you,' because there's a big risk I might not sound convincing.

'Kim, I'm still here, you know. If you need me.'

'I don't.'

'OK,' he says, quietly.

In the hall, on his way out, he looks at the phone off the hook, then at me, but says nothing.

I make dinner, bathe the kids and put them to bed. Or at least I try. Sam wants to play Mr Cushion Mountain.

'What's that?' Never heard of it.

'Da new game Dad showded us,' he announces proudly. 'It's gweat fun. I show you.'

This I've got to see.

They collect pillows and cushions and pile them up on my bed. They fight over who will be Mr Cushion Mountain. Sam wins on the basis that it was his idea to play. Mr Cushion Mountain climbs the mountain of pillows.

'Wedy.'

'Feeling lucky, punk?' Chloe shouts then tries to knock him off the mountain with a pillow.

He screams in delight and clings on.

'Take that, Big Boy,' she shouts.

My laugh is loud and hearty and surprises me as much as them.

Can I allow myself to believe that he's changing? I would so love him to be around to see them grow – to witness Sam putting toothpaste on the brush by himself, Chloe learning to read, spell and ask for real earrings, and Sam eating with a fork (kind of).

My phone starts to vibrate. I tense. And ignore it.

'OK, bedtime.'

They complain, of course.

It takes a while – and three stories – before they finally settle down.

Downstairs I take my phone out. And try not to scream. Hasn't Peter spoken to him? Or has he just not made a difference? When is this going to stop? What will it take to convince Connor that this is getting weird?

I pace the sitting room, searching my mind for a solution.

I stop as one forms in my mind. It involves a lie but it's the only way.

Then I'm texting:

Stop calling me or I'll go to the police. This is harassment. I love Sarah. And I'm back with Ian. So just stop.

I hate threatening him with the police. And I hate lying about Ian. But how else can I make him wake up to himself? He is becoming a borderline stalker. And he needs to know it.

forty

At eleven, I'm locking up when the doorbell rings. I squint through the peephole. It's Ian. And he doesn't look happy. I open up.

'What is it?'

'I've had a call from Connor. You *hypocrite!*'

I feel my cheeks burn. 'Come inside. You'll wake the children.'

He follows me into the sitting room. I close the door behind us.

'You've been at it all along!'

'What?' I whisper.

'You watched me beat myself up, beg for forgiveness… while you were with him all the time!'

'No!'

'You came to my office and *humiliated* me. Have you any idea what that was like? I had to face those people every day until I left.

But I accepted it because I deserved it. And I wanted us all to be together again. But you were with him all the time!'

'No!'

'Did you enjoy watching me grovel? Did you?'

'Can I speak?'

He stops. Finally.

'Do you want a drink?' I ask.

'I want the truth.'

'OK but you have to let me speak. You can't interrupt. It's not black and white.'

'Nothing is,' he says pointedly.

We stand facing each other.

'All right, give me your side.' It's like a dare – give me your side and I'll see if I believe it.

'OK. Firstly, he's lying. I didn't have an affair with him. When I went to London nothing happened. Of course nothing happened, I still loved you. And, like I've told you so many times, it wouldn't have even crossed my mind to think of Connor in that way. But. BUT. When I found out about *you*, something inside me snapped. The most important thing in my life had been ripped apart. I was devastated, lonely, abandoned...'

'But it was you who kicked me out.'

'Please don't interrupt me, Ian. I'm trying to explain. I was here on my own one evening after a particularly bad day. I was drinking. Connor showed up. He said he loved me. I reminded him we were both – technically – married. He seemed to back down. Then he wanted a kiss. Just a kiss. I thought what harm would it do, one kiss. But then, I don't know, things just took over...'

He puts up a hand. 'Enough! Jesus.'

'It happened once. It was a mistake. Not some sordid affair. Our marriage was over – you'd made sure of that. My guilt was for Sarah. Not you. Connor went back to London. That was it.'

'Why would he say you were having an affair?'

If I tell him that Connor has gone borderline psycho, he'll throw it back in my face, say he was right about him all along.

'All right, believe Connor. Doesn't matter to me. I know the truth. I know what happened. I don't need to defend myself to you. It's late, Ian. I'm tired.' I start to walk to the front door.

He follows in baffled silence, all sense of indignant purpose gone.

And as I close the door behind him I think: I don't care. I don't care what he thinks. What I care about is Connor's deception. Our friendship is over. Which probably means I've lost Sarah too – because nothing can ever be explained.

I'm crawling into bed fully dressed when my phone rings. It's Sarah. I panic. He's told her. Or she's found out. Wouldn't be hard – one look at his phone… I stare at the screen, debating whether or not to answer. Then I do. Because I owe it to her.

'He's left me!' she sobs.

'Oh, God.'

'He came home and started shouting. Said he didn't love me.'

'Oh, Sarah.'

'He called me all sorts of things. Said I was a slut and that I cared only for myself and that I treated men like shit. It's not true, I'm not like that.' I hear her taking a long pull on a cigarette. 'He said he doesn't know why he married me.'

'I wish I was there with you.' But that would make me a hypocrite, being there, comforting her, when I cheated on her. If only I could wipe out what happened, make it go away.

'He hit me, Kim.'

I go cold. 'Are you OK? Oh God, Sarah? Tell me you're OK.'

'I'm OK.'

'*Are* you?'

'No.'

'Do you need a doctor?'

'No but I could do with an assassin.'

'Are you injured?'

'No.'

'Are you sure?'

'He hit me hard across the face and I fell. Then he shouted at me over and over. Said it was all my fault. I didn't know what he was talking about. I just crouched on the ground where I landed. Said nothing. Didn't even look at him. I was so afraid, Kim.'

'He'd been drinking.' It's not a question. It's an answer. And I don't know why I didn't think of it before.

'Yes.'

'Where is he now?'

'He stormed out.'

'Where are you?'

'In the apartment.'

'Get out, now. Don't be there when he comes back. Where can you go?'

'I don't know. I've contacts over here but no real friends. I'm so embarrassed. And I'm scared, Kim. Really scared.'

'Get out of the apartment. Get a taxi. Check into a hotel, ask them to get a doctor. Then book the first flight home. Come stay with me, please, Sarah.' I have to make it up to her, make this right.

'But I love him.'

Who invented love? Because they messed up – completely.

'Has he told you about his problem?' I ask.

'What problem?'

'He has a problem with alcohol. He can't drink. If he does and gets upset, he can get violent. He can't help it.'

'He never told me that. Why didn't he tell me?'

'Maybe because he never planned to drink again. Maybe because he thought it was in the past.'

Like I did.

'Why didn't *you* tell me? Warn me?'

'Sarah, I didn't know you were even going out with him not to mind marrying him. As soon as you got together, it was up to Connor to tell you. Anyway, I didn't think it was a problem. He had it under control. For years. And it only ever happened once in his life. He went to a psychologist, gave up booze and got it under control. He can do that again. But that won't happen in a few hours and it won't happen without him getting help. For now, you need to get away. Where is he? Did he say where he was going?'

'I don't know. He said he was going to see the only woman he's ever loved and make her see sense. He said he was a fool not to do it before now.' She breaks down completely.

I feel fear, real fear, creeping up my spine.

'That hurt more than the knock, Kim. That he doesn't love me. He loves someone else. And I never knew. Just like in my book. Ha!' I hear her light another cigarette. 'I didn't know he loved someone else. Did you?' She sounds so suddenly young and innocent.

'Sarah, get out of there now, I mean it.' I should be offering myself the same advice. But where can I go with two children in the middle of the night? I could go to my mother's. But so could he. 'Sarah, are you there?'

'Yes.'

'What are you going to do?'

'What you said.'

'OK. Good. Will you call me when you've seen the doctor?'

'If it's not too late.'

'Call me. I won't be asleep. And don't go back to the apartment.'

'OK.' She sounds defeated.

'Promise?'

'Promise.'

'And Sarah? I'm so sorry.'

'It's not your fault I married a psycho.'

'He's not a psycho. He just can't drink.'

'Still not your fault.'

I want so much to tell her. And I will. As soon as she's safe. 'Sarah, leave now.'

'I'm going.'

'Good. And call me when you get to the hotel.'

I hang up and remember her words. He's coming. To make me see sense. I race to the bathroom to throw up.

Leaning over the loo, I realise with great clarity that I have to check every lock in the house. I have to make sure he can't get in.

I tear around the house, checking doors, locking windows I never usually lock. I close curtains, turn off lights. I check on the children. Sam's mobile of trains casts shadows on the wall and across his face. Chloe looks like she fell asleep dancing, one arm stretched up over her head, the other bent to her hip. It makes her seem more vulnerable than ever. I can't risk it. I can't risk him coming here. I have to do something.

I could have thought of Mum. I could have thought of the police. I could probably have thought of quite a number of options had I not immediately thought of Ian.

The doorbell rings and my heart booms. I steal downstairs by the light of my phone. I peer through the peephole. I can't make out who's there and can't put the light on in case it's Connor. I can hear my heart; at least that's how it feels.

'Kim? It's me,' comes Ian's voice.

My body deflates in relief. I hurry to open the door, then immediately bolt it behind him. I turn on the lights.

'What's going on?' he asks.

'Come inside.'

In the sitting room, I explain everything.

His face softens. 'Why didn't you tell me, earlier, that he was hassling you?'

'Because I thought you'd rub it in.'

'What?'

'Say you were right about him all along.'

He smiles. 'I might have but I'd have still wanted to help.'

'I wouldn't have wanted you to. I wanted to handle it. Then he hit Sarah and I couldn't risk him coming here. I had to think of the children.'

He nods, looks around. 'Have you locked everything?'

'Yeah and double checked a million times.'

'Has he rung?'

'No.'

'OK.' He sits on the edge of a chair, leaning forward, reminding me of the time he asked my father to marry me. And I think: all the things we shared. He looks up from examining the floor. 'Sorry about earlier, about believing him.' He shrugs. 'It made sense. He's always had a thing for you. And I just got so angry, the thought of him with you...' He looks at me with such hurt in his eyes.

'So you know how I felt, how I could have gone to your office.' I bite my lip. 'I did regret it...when I calmed down.'

He looks at me for the longest time. 'I wish we could go back.'

My smile is sad. I feel so tired. So defeated. All the mistakes we made. We sit looking at each other in the sitting room that was ours, the home that was ours, thinking of the life that was ours.

'Do you want a drink?' I ask.

He shakes his head. 'I'll have a coffee though. Might need a stimulant.' He smiles.

I smile back. I give him that. Then I head for the kitchen.

'Do you think he'll come tonight?' he asks, following me in.

'I don't know but, from what Sarah said, if he can get a flight he probably will.'

He nods.

'I think it'll be OK. Once he sees you're here.'

He looks doubtful. 'Might help if I'd ever been to a gym.'

I smile. 'It's not that. I told him we were back together – so that he'd leave me alone.'

'Oh.'

'If he sees you here, he'll probably wake up to himself and stop drinking.'

'So you want me to pretend we're together?'

'If you don't mind.'

'I don't mind.' The look he gives me makes me turn back to the kettle. And I wish – so hard – that I could just hate him.

'What if he turns up tomorrow?' he asks.

I turn and put my hand to my forehead. 'I hadn't thought that far ahead.'

'I can sleep on the couch, take the day off work, stick around. I'm winding things up in there anyway. I have a few days due.'

My shoulders fall in relief. 'Thanks, Ian. I really appreciate it.' So formal.

From the kitchen table, he picks up one of Sam's trains. Percy. His favourite. He runs his finger over it. Then he looks at me.

'This is my fault. If I hadn't been so bloody stupid, none of this would have happened.'

'Maybe we should forget about faults.' Whoa. Where did that come from?

He looks at me with such hope that I panic.

'Ian, just so we're clear… If Connor comes and I say I love you that doesn't mean it's true.'

The hope dies in his eyes.

And I'm sorry again. Confused. 'I better go call Sarah. See if she's all right.'

He nods. 'OK if I take the couch?'

'Do you want the sleeping bag?'

'Yeah, I'll get it.' He smiles sadly. 'Night.'

'Night, Ian. And thank you.' In the hall, I turn back.

He's running the train over the table.

'By the way. I love Mr Cushion Mountain.'

His smile warms my heart. If only love was enough.

Sarah is in a hotel and sounds much better.

'I'll fly over in the morning and stay with my parents. It's funny but I really need to see them.' She sounds teary.

'Will you call me when you get there? We could meet up somewhere.' I have to tell her. No matter what Peter says.

'I'll call you when I land.'

Oh God. Maybe Peter's right. Maybe I'll only hurt her.

forty-one

'Dad! Dad! Saaaam, it's Dad!' Chloe shouts up the stairs. 'Dad's here!'

Sam bursts from his room.

'Dad's here!' he shouts, his little legs taking him down the stairs so fast he looks like a train. If only he knew – he'd be delighted.

I follow him into the sitting room to find them both on top of a smiling Ian.

'Are you back from the hotel? Is your holiday over, Dad?' Chloe asks excitedly.

'I'm just here for a little visit, honey. Do you still have tickles?'

She squeals in terror and excitement.

'Me too, me too,' Sam shouts.

But he underestimates his powers of control and has an 'accident'.

Ian carries him upstairs, cleans him up and puts on his Sunny Side Up uniform.

A voice in my head tells me that things would be different if I took him back now. Another voice asks how long that would last.

The kids' happiness at their father making breakfast breaks my heart.

Ian comes with us on the school run. I call Fonsie to see if it's OK to work on the proposal from home. I set up on the kitchen table while Ian empties the dishwasher and puts the bin out. Then he joins me with his laptop. And coffee for two.

I focus on the proposal. The ideas just keep coming, with them a genuine enthusiasm to implement them. Still, every noise from outside has me jump. The post being delivered. The bins being emptied. I look at Ian.

'If he's going to come, let him come now before we pick up the kids.'

He gives that thought then says, 'If he doesn't, we should take them off for the day.'

I nod.

'We could go to Tara.'

With all its connotations. And yet, we can't stay here. 'OK.'

They are so excited to see their father again, they fling themselves at him.

'Dad! Dad! What are you doing here?' Chloe asks.

'We've brought a picnic. We're going to Tara.'

'Yaay.'

In the car, my mind plays good-cop-bad-cop:

He's really trying. The kids love him. I love him. Take him back.

He'll do it again.

He won't.

He will.

You really think he'll risk losing his family again?

If he thinks I'm a walkover, he will.

Give him a chance. We all make mistakes. You of all people know that.

But things will go back to the way they were. Communication will break down.

Only if you let it.

He'll work too hard. Lose interest in us.

He won't.

He won't help around the house.

Get help. You've an income now.

I'll get help but I'm not taking him back.

'I better stay the night,' Ian says at ten that evening.

I grimace. 'I feel like a bit of an eejit.'

He smiles. 'I'll go in the morning.'

Part of me doesn't want him to go at all. The weak part.

'The kids will be delighted,' I say.

He looks at me as if to say, 'Just the kids?'

I look away, don't trust myself not to. 'Do you need to get a suit and stuff for tomorrow?'

He thinks about that. 'Probably should. Will you be OK for twenty minutes?'

'Yeah.'

'Lock the door. If he calls, don't let him in. Just ring me and I'll turn around.'

'OK.'

He's gone five minutes when the doorbell rings.

And I think, typical, bloody typical. Then I think, Oh God. He's been watching the house, waiting for Ian to go!

The doorbell goes again.

I force myself to peer out.

It's Sarah! I fling back the door and rush out to hug her.

'Sarah, thank God. Are you OK? Come in, come in.' I hurry her inside. 'Jesus. Look at you.' There's a massive bruise on her cheek and no make up can hide that black eye.

I show her into the kitchen. 'Drink?'

She nods.

I get the whiskey out. And we sit at the table.

'Did you go to the police?'

She nods. 'They filed a report. It will help with the divorce.'

'Oh.'

'Oh what?'

'I don't know. You love him.'

'He doesn't love me.'

'It's just the drink…'

'Kim, I'm too long in the tooth to take abuse from anyone. Even Connor. I've thought about it all night. No man's worth it. I might have given him a chance if he loved me but he doesn't. And I don't want to be with a man who doesn't want to be with me. You can understand that.'

I nod.

'What's that?' she asks.

'Oh it's just a proposal I'm working on.'

'You're *working*?'

'Sorry. Didn't I tell you? I've been offered a part-time job in an art gallery.'

'No, you didn't tell me. We haven't spoken in ages. You never call me back.'

'I'm sorry. I don't know, I didn't want to bother you with everything.' Or talk to Connor. 'But forget that, what about you, what are *you* going to do?'

'Divorce him. Move on. Should never have married in the first place.'

'I'm sorry things haven't worked out. I really am.'

'Plenty of fish – who knows better than me?' Despite a smile she looks heartbroken.

'Sarah, I have to tell you something about Connor…'

A loud thump comes from upstairs, followed by a cry.

'What was *that*?' Sarah asks.

'One of the kids must have fallen out of bed. Back in a sec.'

I run upstairs.

It's Sam. He's fine. Asleep on the carpet. I pick him up gently and place him back on his *Thomas The Tank Engine* pillow. I'm smoothing back his hair when I hear the doorbell.

'I'll get it,' Sarah calls.

Oh God. What'll she think when she sees Ian? He'll know not to tell her about Connor won't he?

I run. I'm halfway down the stairs when I see her take a step back from the door. Then I see who's there.

'What are *you* doing here?' Connor asks her.

Sarah turns and stares up at me, as the truth dawns. 'It's *you*? *You're* the one he loves?'

'I was just going to tell you.' It sounds weak, even to me.

'Kim?' Connor calls. He looks crazed.

'Connor. You need to go see Peter. You've been drinking.' If I can just get to the door. Shut it. Call Ian.

'Bitch,' Sarah spits at me then runs from the house.

Oh God, he's in.

'Get out, Connor,' I say as calmly as I can. 'Get out now before I call the police.' Only problem is, my phone is in the sitting room.

'You know you love me,' he says, closing the door behind him.

'I love Ian and he'll be back any second.'

He starts towards me. This is my friend for as long as I can remember, a vegetarian, for Christ's sake. Do I continue down the stairs, walk boldly past him to my phone? Will he let me? Or do I reverse, show weakness? In the end, I stay where I am. 'Get out of my house,' I say in a low voice that always works with children.

He stops.

So I advance.

But then he begins to stumble towards me.

I'm not going to make the sitting room. I'm not going to get past him. So I stop again.

'I told you. I'm back with Ian.'

'Where is he then?' he demands, looking around in an exaggerated manner.

'He'll be here any minute.' I look at the door. Any second. Please Ian. Walk in the bloody door. Please.

Connor laughs. 'Really? Or is he with her? Come on, Kim – I thought you had more sense.'

'He won't be happy to see you here, Connor.'

'Ooooh, I'm really scared now. Look, I'm shaking.' He holds out his hands, spreads his fingers and shakes them exaggeratedly.

The front door opens. Ian takes in the scene.

'Connor was just leaving,' I say to him.

They face each other.

Connor smiles. 'Well if it isn't the prodigal husband.'

'Connor, you're not welcome here,' Ian says calmly, firmly. 'And don't call my wife again or you'll have the police to deal with. They take harassment very seriously.'

'Oooh, Ian, you're frightening me with all those big words.'

'Just go,' Ian says with just the right degree of tired exasperation.

'Look who's talking? Mr Bang The Boss.' Connor looks at me triumphantly.

'You can't talk,' I say.

He smiles. 'Neither can you. As it happens.'

Before I know what's happened, Connor is on the ground, nursing his jaw. Ian is holding his fist, looking as surprised as the rest of us.

I take a deep breath. Here goes.

'We all made mistakes, Connor. Ian is sorry and I forgive him. We're back together. You should look to your own marriage now before you lose it. You've hurt Sarah so much. I still can't believe you hit her. You've no idea how much she loved you. And she doesn't love easily. You need to go and see Peter before it's too late. Before this goes any further.'

Connor stares at me as he pulls himself up off the floor. It's as if I've just told him something he didn't know. He pales. 'I hit her? I hit Sarah?'

'Yes, you hit your wife. Maybe that's what you should focus on for a while.'

He runs his hands through his hair looking like he's just woken up. 'Christ.'

'Call Peter before you do anything else. Sort this out. Please.'

And he just leaves, walks out, holding his head.

I'm shaking. Even my kneecaps are trembling.

'You OK?' Ian asks.

I nod.

'Stay here. I'm just going to get Sarah from the car.'

'Sarah?'

'She was leaving as I was driving in; I told her to wait in the car.'

'She won't have, though.' I know Sarah.

'We'll see. Close the door behind me.'

Sarah won't meet my eyes. I want to tell her everything but Ian asks me to get her a glass of water. While I'm gone, he sits her down and starts to explain. It sounds better coming from him and I'm so grateful. I hand Sarah the glass and am surprised when she takes it. I don't know whether to stay or go, so I sit quietly out of the way.

'I'm so sorry, Sarah,' I say when Ian finishes.

'Did you think about me even *once*?' she asks.

'As soon as I did, I stopped. I'm sorry. I felt terrible. We both did. We wanted to tell you but Connor's psychologist said not to – that it would hurt you too much. Connor went back to London to make your marriage work but at some point he must have started drinking. He loves you, Sarah, he really does. He thinks you're great. It's just the drink. If he goes back to see Peter...'

'You bitch,' she whispers. 'Pretending to be sympathetic...'

'I *was* sympathetic. Genuinely. And I was about to tell you when Sam fell out of bed.'

'You know, I don't have many friends. I'm too brash for most people. But I thought *you* were my friend, Kim. You fucked my husband then pretended to comfort me. That's all I need to know. I don't care what you were going through, how drunk you were. I can't forgive you, Kim. I can never forgive you.' She gets up.

So do I. 'Sarah. I'd never do anything to hurt you. I don't

know how it happened. Everything seemed to just rush out of control.' I hear myself sounding like Ian did. So I know it's useless. How can I expect Sarah to forgive me when I'm standing here unable to forgive Ian? I bow my head and whisper, 'I'm sorry.'

She starts to leave.

'Let me give you a lift,' Ian says. 'Where are you staying?'

'With my parents.' She sighs. 'It's OK, I'll get a taxi.'

'No you won't. Come on.' He puts an arm around her.

She doesn't argue.

Ian turns to me. 'Lock the door.'

I nod. But who'd want to come in? I've lost everyone.

To keep busy, I light a fire. It's just taking hold when Ian returns.

'She hates me,' I say.

He smiles. 'A bit.'

'It's not funny.'

'It's not the end of the world either.'

I give him a look.

He holds it. 'You're ultimately a good person. She'll see that when she calms down. And if she doesn't, you're still a good person.'

That surprises me. 'Thank you.'

'My pleasure.' He sits on the couch. Blows out a breath. Then he looks at me. 'Were you scared?'

I nod. 'You?'

He smiles. 'Damn right I was.'

I find myself smiling. 'I hope he'll be OK.'

He thinks about that. Then, like he's letting go, he says, 'Me too.' He clears his throat. 'Because he's ultimately a good person.'

'He is.'

He looks at me significantly. 'We all are.'

Admitting that is the biggest step of all.

'I should probably stay tonight. In case he comes back.'

'He won't be back, Ian.'

'No. But did you see the kids' faces this morning when they saw me here?'

God. This is so hard.

'Just for tonight,' he says.

'I'll get the sleeping bag.'

I stare into the airing cupboard. Socks, vests, towels, sheets, clothes lie knotted up together. Messy. Not folded, not perfect. Yet somehow we manage. I think of Mum and the compromises she made, the patience she had, and how, in the end, she got what she wanted. She was not too big for a deal.

I go downstairs and into the kitchen. I find a pen and paper, then sit at the table. I start to write:

If you want to stay longer than a night, these are my conditions:
1. *We live day by day. As friends.*
2. *We see someone. No expectations. No assumptions.*
3. *We parent fifty-fifty.*
4. *We communicate.*
5. *We discuss problems.*
6. *We listen.*
7. *We go out every Friday night. Just to talk and remember who we were.*
8. *Unless we decide to separate, we are still technically married. If you are EVER unfaithful, deal over.*

I take a deep breath and stand.

In the sitting room, wordlessly, I hand him The Deal.

He looks at me in surprise, then reads in silence.

He puts the sheet of paper aside, then stands. He looks down at me for what seems the longest time, then takes me in his arms and squeezes me tight with gratitude. Then he says one word.

'Deal.'

THE END

acknowledgements

Thank you, Nicola Russell, you star, for inspiring me to take the first steps on this adventure. Thank you and hugs to the very special Karen and Liam Lorenzo for my cover; I saw that photo and fell in love with it. Huge thanks to Sandy Brugh, Diane Galburt, Bev Morris, Laura Tyrrell and Nikki Weijdom for your eagle eyes and willingness to help. Massive thanks to everyone who advised me on titles. This has been my most collaborative work; and I love that.

Big thanks and appreciation to these lovely writers: Colette Caddle, Celia Carlisle, Sally Clements, Helena Close, Judi Curtin, Catherine Daly, Claire Dowling, Maria Duffy, Suzy Duffy, Catherine Dunne, Laura Elliot, Eleanor Fitzsimons, Hazel Gaynor, Jean Grainger, Niamh Greene, Claire Hennessy, Michelle Jackson, Sheena Lambert, Hazel Larkin, Ruth Long, Zoe Miller, Clodagh Murphy, Morag Prunty, Tali Roland, Catherine Ryan Howard, Louise Ryan McCarthy, Barbara Scully, Mel Sherratt, Niamh O'Connor, Deirdre Maria Sullivan, Jane Travers and Ciara Winkleman for their advice, support and encouragement.

Thank you to everyone who has taken the time to review my books, highlight them on social media and recommend them to friends. Hugely appreciate your support. Particular thanks to Frank Burns, Margaret Bonass Madden, Alison Cain, Geraldine Finnegan Gaul, Charles Hale, Valerie Judge, John Ivory, Louise Kelly, Samantha Mackey, Michelle Moloney King, Patricia Kieran, Liz Magee, Monica Leal Arcas, Helen Shaw and Claire Rudd.

Thanks to my family, as always, for being supportive, brutal and humorous at the same time.

Above all, thank you to my readers. Without you, there would be no books.

Printed in Great Britain
by Amazon